White Lightning

White Lightning

TRUTH IS A POWERFUL ELIXIR

Minton Sparks

THOMAS NELSON
Since 1798

NASHVILLE DALLAS MEXICO CITY RIO DE JANEIRO BEIJING

Published in Nashville, Tennessee, by Thomas Nelson. Thomas Nelson is a registered trademark of Thomas Nelson, Inc.

Thomas Nelson, Inc. titles may be purchased in bulk for educational, business, fund-raising, or sales promotional use. For information, please e-mail SpecialMarkets@ThomasNelson.com.

Publisher's Note: This novel is a work of fiction. Names, characters, places, and incidents are either products of the author's imagination or used fictitiously. All characters are fictional, and any similarity to people living or dead is purely coincidental.

Library of Congress Cataloging-in-Publication Data

Sparks, Minton.
    White lightning / Minton Sparks.
      p. cm.
    ISBN 978-1-59554-263-2 (hardcover)
    1. Beauty operators—Fiction. 2. Nashville (Tenn.)—Fiction. 3. Domestic fiction. I. Title.
PS3619.P354W47 2008
813'.6—dc22

2008001640

Printed in the United States of America

08 09 10 11 12 QW 6 5 4 3 2 1

For Jonas Sidney Sparks on his "100th"

When the music is dark, it works through dissonance and
    harsh notes;
like underpainting their beauty is slow to reveal itself but it
    does ultimately dawn.
It frees a space to let in lightness.

—JOHN O'DONOHUE

One

Doris Jenkins was extremely tender-headed, so I eased the aqua rods out of her hair, careful not to tug too hard else she'd holler out. I liked to trim Doris's ends before rinsing out her perm. The snipped ammonia-smelling wisps of hair were tickling the tops of my feet when the call came through. I had to make it to Momma and Daddy's house as quick as I could. Left Doris stranded in my swivel chair examining the cuticles on her arthritic hands. Poor lady looked like a somber poodle in a black cape sitting there.

"You're gonna have to rinse it and comb it out yourself, Doris; my grandmother's dying." I lifted my jean jacket off the hall tree and jerked open the door.

"Grab you a clean comb out of that blue rinse water."

"What?" She didn't hear me over the noise of the door bells.

"I said, after you rinse, grab you a clean comb out of that blue water in the sink."

I'd left my tennis shoes out in the car, so I had to run barefoot across the parking lot.

Friday afternoon traffic was bumper-to-bumper on Summer Avenue heading east out of Memphis at five o'clock. One cloud, a misshapen rabbit running at full tilt, hung in the early evening sky. Had plenty of daylight savings time left for me to make it before dark. I took Covington Pike all the way to the Brownsville exit before cutting over to I-40 to save a little time. Turning the corner at the Shell Station, an empty Bud Light rolled up under the brake pedal. Fumbling on the floorboard for the loose bottle, I felt wet drops on my car mat. Blood dripped from beneath a flap of skin on my big toe. Must've sliced it walking to the car. The cut wasn't deep but it was jagged. I grabbed a pair of white gym shorts loose in the backseat to stop the bleeding.

For a split second I thought about pulling over and calling Darrell, but the white paint in the middle of the road kept clicking by. *Where's my music?* I groped the knobs on the dashboard and found an empty hole where my radio reliably rested. *What?* My eyes darted back and forth, back and forth, from the road to the dark hole, keeping time with the click click of the blinker light—*don't die don't die don't die.* I must've tripped my blinker whipping out of the parking lot. *I'll be damn.* Copper wires dangled like raw nerves from the socket of a pulled tooth. The tooth in this case being my JVC radio, a wedding present from Darrell six years ago. The Reese's Pieces, McDonalds' sacks, and old dream catcher hanging off the rearview mirror, were now evidence at a crime scene. Some idiot had worked a coat hanger or Slim Jim down into the passenger side window and ripped off my radio while

I'd been working. The black rubber, formerly sealing the window, was flapping in the wind. *Don't die don't die.* Once I cut the heater off and got the blinker settled I resigned myself to the high-pitched whine whistling in the vandalized window. For the rest of the ride I couldn't decide what to think about.

Daddy was disappointed when I decided to go to beauty college right out of high school. "Smart as you are, Penny Sue," he said, "you could be the first Pritchett to get a degree."

Even though the focus was on fixing hair and painting nails, I still liked the idea of beauty school. Just saying it made me feel good. Jebo understood. She said she felt the same way about her music.

"I wouldn't take anything for the way my music makes me feel," she'd say. "Not a million dollars, not a great big house, nothing."

Beauty never touched Momma. It was like she was immune to its power. She didn't even like flowers. Can you imagine not liking flowers? When I was a little girl I'd cut out pretty pictures from *Ladies' Home Journal* magazine and paste them onto card stock as gifts to cheer her up.

"Thank you, hon," Momma'd say flatly, her fingers wiggling down toward my voice for the homemade card, her eyes glued to her television story, *As the World Turns.* Then without missing any of the drama, she'd spin around on the stool and carelessly slide my picture into the chewing gum drawer beside the kitchen sink.

My artwork often featured what they referred to in the

magazine as the "Florida room"—that giant wicker fan, those soft pastel colors, and all that sunshine streaming in the sparkling windows, the housewives in the photos beaming in the midst of all the splendor. Made me question the power of floral throw pillows—could they really cause a mother to smile down at her daughter the way the picture showed?

Momma either neglected beauty or never had an eye for it in the first place. The walls in our house were painted hospital beige all my life. Most of our furniture leaned toward putty blue. I think the colors matched her moods. Damped down.

As I pulled up to the curve, I thought about how that house was full of hideous furniture, all of it overstuffed and slightly flawed. Daddy'd brought home "seconds" every six months or so from his furniture store. He'd deliver them himself—roar up over the curb and into the front yard in the delivery truck—busted the oil pan twice best I remember. He'd honk the horn for Momma, Jebo, and me to come out and help him drag whatever new ugly piece of furniture he'd brought home in the front door.

"Get that blame truck off my grass, Porter," Momma said every time he did it.

Sometimes he'd carry off the existing couch into a storage shed outside, but more often than not he crammed the new piece of furniture right on into that front room that he called our den. I never realized how crowded our house was until I moved out of it.

Momma's prized grandfather clock boom-chimed as I pushed open the paneled front door. After six strikes, dead silence.

"Daddy?!" I ran and called up the narrow carpeted stairway to the converted attic. "Daddy, you up there?"

Daddy knelt on the floor beside Jebo, dabbing her brow with a cool washrag and holding her paper-thin hand. His white sock poked through a hole worn in the sole of his Weejuns. (He still wore dress pants and a sports jacket around the house though he'd sold Pritchett's Furniture a month ago.) His soft eyes, swollen and red, turned toward my voice.

"Jebo's gone, Penny Sue. Couldn't have been no more than two minutes ago."

In the corner, Momma fidgeted in the white wicker rocking chair beneath pictures of Grand Ole Opry stars Jebo had taped to the dark-paneled walls. An oscillating fan on the bedside table swiveled its neck around the room, a continuous final exhale.

"Is this too summer-y?" Momma looked at me and said. I swear that's exactly what she said, not "Hi," "Bye," or "Kiss my foot," but *"Is this too summer-y?"* Holding her flower-print skirt out at an angle like she was about to perform a seated curtsy or something. While my Jebo was growing cold in the bottom bunk, beneath a sweetheart quilt. I ignored Momma's comment and went over to hug Daddy's neck.

"I'm so sorry, Daddy." I turned and whispered, "Momma, can you get me a Band-Aid?"

She scurried out the door, happy to have something to do. Over on the far wall, beside the one window in the room, hung Jebo's prize Gibson guitar—the narrowest part of the neck hanging between two nails. I crouched down beside Daddy on the sea of yellow shag carpet, where no doubt silverfish swam, patting his burly back and cautioning him not to rear up and hit his head on the angled attic ceiling. Didn't realize I'd bit through my lip until I tasted the blood. After that, neither of us said another word as he covered Jebo's face with the quilt and then gently traced the pattern with his finger.

Come to think of it, it was in that rich silence that I first heard the sound track come on. I looked around to see if Momma had flipped on the radio, but she'd tiptoed downstairs. The song playing in my head was "The Queen Anne's Revenge," a sorrowful fiddle tune played on mandolin. I like to think that the music gave Jebo comfort as she crossed over to the other side.

Two

The funeral director, Vic Victory, rested his prepared statements upon his beach-ball belly. His brush cut suggested military affiliation. He'd take a nip every now and then off a small silver flask. At first I thought it was breath freshener. He'd bury it back into his suit pocket after each little sip. His eulogy wandered. Made you wonder if it was recycled. Momma said he might as well have been burying a rank stranger.

I had prepared some things I wanted to say about Jebo, but when I stood up, Momma yanked me back down in the seat and hot-whispered, "Sit down! Don't you get up there and make a fool of yourself, Penny Sue."

"What?" I mouthed.

"I said, sit down." She snapped her fingers and pointed to the pew beneath me. "Trying to make a spectacle of yourself in front of everybody."

In the years since I'd left home, Momma had not lost her ability to sap my strength with a single remark. Slowly I lowered my butt back onto the navy cushion. I should have known not to sit by her. Grover Messick, the Rexall pharmacist who occupied the row in front of us, cut his eyes at Momma and then harrumphed back around to face the mahogany casket. Wasn't nothing but fourteen hairs on his shiny bald head. I counted them over and over as I smoldered in my seat.

The only personal touch in the service was when Daddy and his brother and sister, Uncle Billy and Aunt Edna, sang a practiced "How Great Thou Art." I couldn't see Aunt Edna's face good because it was partially hidden behind a wreath of flowers on a three-pronged stand. Mr. Victory leaned over to join in with a high tenor harmony, but Aunt Edna put her hand up like a stop sign and "shushed" him. After the song, while making his way back to his seat, Mr. Victory's big belly knocked over the biggest flower arrangement—must have cost a fortune—white carnations adhered to a podium with a dangling white telephone receiver spilling over the top. Black letters on a white sign read "Jesus Called."

Jebo lay in the casket, which was open head to toe, wearing a hot pink pantsuit and black patent-leather pumps with a bow. Whoever did her hair oughtta been shot; the curl had fallen out and it lay limp beneath a matching pillbox hat cocked off to one side of her head. She looked a little like a drunken sailor.

"Is it hot in here to y'all?" Momma tried to get me to answer, but I wouldn't. My guess was that Momma picked out that pink pantsuit as payback. It looked absolutely ridiculous. She never liked Jebo a bit, though I would have drawn family fire if I'd mentioned a word about it.

Momma interrupted my thoughts. "Penny Sue, when we get back to the house don't run off and hide in your old room

with one of your books; we need you to put on a brave face."
Momma thought I was uppity because I liked to read.

After the service folks filed out into the emerald green
entryway of the funeral home. The funeral director's wife,
Jerry Ann, quickly passed out typed-up directions on small
slips of green paper to the cemetery three blocks away. She
got to passing so fast she dropped the entire stack on the foyer
floor. (Evidently another funeral was coming in right behind
us.) Uncle Billy hitched up his suit pants and struggled down
to help her.

"Hey, stranger," Jerry Ann said as she caught eyes with
Uncle Billy on his way back up. (They dated pretty hot and
heavy back in high school.) Jerry Ann had to be pushing sixty.
She still looked like a million bucks, though, in that expensive
charcoal suit and ankle-strap heels. Her Navajo-black hair
hung down her back gathered in a big silver barrette with a
lake-shaped turquoise stone set in the middle.

Momma couldn't help herself as she scraped by me going
out the door. "Remember, we live in a dry county, Penny Sue."
Then without even a breath as a segue she added, "Her skin's
mighty bronzed for this late in October, if you ask me."

As a teenager, I always liked Jerry Ann, and Vic, her husband, too. Vic Victory coached my church league basketball
team. That was back before he took over his daddy's funeral
home. Victory's Funeral Home sponsored our team jerseys.
The logo, "Victory!" was written inside a cartoonish casket. Bet
you Jerry Ann had something to do with the design. Momma
insisted I wear a plain red T-shirt to the games, said the jerseys

were "irrelevant." I think she meant "irreverent." Before the funeral, I hadn't seen Jerry Ann in ten years. Her mouth flew open wide in mock surprise when she saw me.

"Oooh, I'm so sorry about your Jebo, Penny Sue. I know y'all were real close."

"Thanks, Jerry Ann."

"I like your hair long, Penny Sue."

Suddenly I remembered the time she lowered the back lip of her bathing suit and showed me her tatoo in the dressing room at the Cedars of Lebanon State Park swimming pool. Her husband's initials, VV, branded in blue-black ink high on her left hip. I would have mistaken it for the letter W had she not carefully explained her show-and-tell. I'd never been so embarrassed in all my life. I couldn't look her in the eye the rest of the season.

Somehow the memory emboldened me. I dragged Jerry Ann over into the corner of the foyer to unload some of what I had planned to say during the funeral service. "You know, Jebo had my daddy when she was seventeen years old."

Great-uncle Frank picked his walker up over his head in order to squeeze by us and get out the door. A tennis ball fell off one walker leg.

"Just a baby herself." Jerry Ann opened her eyes real wide and feigned interest at the same time she leaned around me to pass out cemetery directions.

She wasn't hardly listening, but somehow I couldn't stop myself and kept right on describing Jebo. "She seemed like everybody else's grandmomma, you know? Look at her!

Thinning gray hair, plump above the elbows, and had those murky eyes where the sharp edges of blue iris and black pupil had run together."

"Is that so?" Jerry Ann was straddling irritation and pity.

"Except she could beat the dog out of her guitar, Jerry Ann! She'd wear these red rhinestone cowboy boots to the supper table and she loved to play bingo and slots at the Moose Lodge, but otherwise she could have been any other old woman in our town."

"Quite a character. Will you excuse me for just a minute?" Jerry Ann held up her pointer finger like something had just occurred to her. Next thing I know she's heading outside to console my uncle Billy beside the gaping door of the black hearse. His face was beet red.

But I wasn't done. I wanted to tell her more. I wanted to tell her that in Jebo's room some old-time station was always playing—country standards, like "Walking the Floor Over You," or "Roll in My Sweet Baby's Arms," wafting through the window screens. Didn't matter what song it was, the style and the ache of their whine and twang captured me. Jebo's white rectangular radio stayed glued to the AM channel out of Nashville. The silver antenna pointed east, away from her west Tennessee flatlands.

I longed to tell Jerry Ann or anybody who'd listen that Jebo taught me, "Music stirs the pot of a heavy heart, Penny Sue. It teaches you a different way to hold all your sorrow. Sometimes even helps you sidle up to the sacred." I especially ached to say, but I didn't get to, that I always imagined Jebo's soul had a certain shape. I'd felt it. Her soul had the shape of an eighth note; a dark round part attached to a wild waving flagstaff.

Momma's gloved fist thumped the car window from inside the shiny, white limousine. But I stood there staring at the black hearse that held the body of my Jebo. She flapped her hand and mouthed, "Hurry up and get in this car." Aunt Edna, her cigarette drooping out the side of her mouth, sat up tall in the backseat beside her. *Over my dead body*, I thought and pointed with my funeral program toward my red Chevette in the back of the parking lot, the paint faded to the color of tomato soup. My clogs cloppity-clopped like shod horses on the hot pavement. Jebo would have noticed the rhythm of the sound.

There was a certain rhythm to the way Jebo spoke, like she was singing, especially when she got to telling her stories. I say "her stories"; I was related to most of the characters, but she hung onto and exaggerated the details. Like the triangular shape of Reverend Cutie Wallace's special shoe he wore on his clubfoot, or the way my cousin Hubert folded and then pinned up his shirtsleeve on his amputated arm. I can see her plain as day in that wool-weave recliner in the den, flanked by a white pump bottle of Jergens lotion to her left and a large cup of hot coffee to her right, laughing to herself before she launched into the one about my daddy's tenth birthday party.

The story played out in my mind like a movie as I slammed shut the car door, turned the key, and eased in front of a silver Eldorado to join the funeral procession over to the Pineview Cemetery. Jebo's older twin sisters, Durrell and Maydelle, had on new handmade, daisy-print lavender dresses with wide, pointy collars. Even though Momma said they looked tacky, I thought they were real pretty. The hem of Durrell's fancy dress once caught fire on the birthday candles. Jebo would get so tickled in the telling she'd have to take her glasses off and lay them in her lap to dab her wet eyes. She loved the part when my daddy, first day in double digits, accidentally threw the Bacardi-spiked pitcher of punch on them, instead of the lemonade, to douse the fire. Of course, the alcohol only inspired the flame; half the birthday party took turns up under cold water in the claw-foot bathtub.

Three

Nobody but Jebo understood why I'd married Darrell Sykes. I'm not sure anybody else could. I nearly chewed her ear off about him the first night I came home from Ross's Barber College over in Memphis.

The swing chain clanked as we rocked on the porch. A light mist fell in the yard. She'd had a tooth pulled that morning, and her head was wrapped in a red bandanna. Gauze filled her lower jaw.

"Pressure's dropping, Penny Sue. My guitar won't hardly hold a tune with this rain that's come on," she said. Her dark brown Gibson rested in her lap, her plump arm protectively slung over the top of the body.

She let me talk as long as I needed.

"I shaved my first head this morning during 8:30 class, Jebo. Nicked this fella's lily-white scalp twice with the straight razor. He was scared stiff—never moved a muscle after I slathered on the cream. That poor boy walked out with two pieces of toilet paper stuck to his skull. I couldn't keep my mind on what I was doing, Jebo. All I can think about is Darrell Sykes."

Jebo shook a Camel from her crumpled pack of cigarettes, flicked her pink see-through lighter and cupped the fire up toward the tobacco. I waited until she'd blown a thick cloud of smoke up across a gauzy moon.

"Darrell's got a day job at the IHOP out in Whitehaven where Elvis Presley lived. Says he wants to be a famous singer one day."

"Can he sing?"

"He has a real sweet voice. I never met anybody like him, Jebo. Remember me telling you how much I've always wanted to see the bald eagles over at Reelfoot Lake?"

"A million times," she mused.

"Well, Darrell carried me over there last weekend. Made it a big surprise and everything. I was staying at Aunt Kate and Uncle Bubba's for the weekend. He strutted up to their door carrying one of those big buckets of KFC. He'd written 'RFL or Bust' with soap on the back window of his metallic blue pickup. When we got over on the highway he hummed what I thought was Eric Clapton's hit 'Wonderful Tonight,' but I couldn't hear good over the roar of the road. When I asked if he'd serenade me properly he immediately hit his right turn signal, pulled over onto the shoulder, wrestled the gearshift into park, threw his head back and closed his eyes to sing, 'Oh my darlin' you look wonderful tonight.' I guess he sang better with his eyes closed. So best not to drive and sing, right?"

"I guess so," Jebo said.

"'How 'bout that?' he asked. His head craning over his left shoulder watching the traffic, trying to safely time his reentry into the flow of cars. I knew that there was more resting on my response than the casual way he asked the question. It was like he needed to know what I thought of his singing before we could go any further.

"I made up something. Told him I loved it.

"After that we listened to a gospel station out of Jackson for a while." Jebo smiled, like that vulnerable picture of Darrell caused a memory of her own, then nudged me with her shoulder to say more.

"We pulled into the parking lot at twilight. His engine *tick tick ticked* after he shut it off. Not a soul around but us."

"Did Aunt Kate try to take y'all's picture? She'll embarrass you to death if you let her."

"No, don't interrupt me, Jebo."

"All right."

"Darrell told me to take off my glasses. I thought a kiss was coming, but all he honestly wanted was to clean them. Fogged the lenses up with his breath and wiped them off with the tail of his T-shirt—turns out my glasses were filthy."

"I love the little details, Penny Sue."

"I felt a tick crawl up under my jeans."

"A tick?"

"Shush, I'm kiddin'. Your tooth okay?"

"I'm fine."

"Anyhow, Darrell held my hand as we walked across the grass toward the lake. The few leaves left on the trees were dry, brittle and brown. I saw him out of the corner of my eye watching every move I made. The light was leaving the sky.

Clouds floated like cotton balls behind his head. He's got a good head of thick hair."

Jebo circled her hand for me to keep going.

"When we got close to the lake, Darrell pointed out a blue heron on a cottonwood limb, cranking its wings before lifting off. He couldn't believe that I'd never seen a heron before."

"I wish we could have traveled more when you were little," Jebo interjected. I kept talking.

"That long-beaked bird flew off low, hovering above the water, like flying over glass. Its dark reflection made me feel . . . I don't know. Homesick."

"Homesick?" she said, her neck and head shaped like her question.

"Yeah, but homesick for somewhere I've never been. Let me finish. I slipped off my shoes and socks and stuck my bare feet into the water; minnows scattered ever-which-a-way. I wished the frogs would have shut up, but everything else was perfect. The twelve-pack we brought sat in the car and got hot.

"This is the part that killed me, Jebo. Darrell got down on one knee and broke the surface of the water with his hand. His face turned real serious, and he didn't say anything for a long time while he tapped his lips with the tips of his fingers. I couldn't imagine what he was going to say, but I didn't want to interrupt whatever he was thinking."

Jebo thrummed a G chord and then stopped immediately the sound with her hand.

"I'm sorry. It just sounded to me like a G-chord moment," Jebo said.

"What he said seemed to come out of someone else's mouth. I promise these were his exact words, 'This place loves you too, Penny Sue.'"

The fire on Jebo's cigarette had burned down to the filter. She flicked it into the bushes beside the porch. It was one of the few times I've seen her lost for words.

"I promise I'm not making this up, Jebo. He dipped his finger in the lake and drew a cross on my forehead like he was baptizing me. As the water ran down my face like a tear he said it again.

"'All this beauty loves you back. Sometimes places that we love, love us too.'"

Jebo's head hung down toward the hole in her guitar. She began to fingerpick a melody. So faint, I could barely hear it. Everything else I said was over the top of her song.

"I can't figure out why what he said got to me. But it's like I got mad. Maybe I was mad at myself for needing to hear it so much. Do you know what I mean, Jebo?"

Jebo stared at her strings, kept right on plucking out the tune. I wondered if my story touched a nerve, but I couldn't make myself stop.

"He sat down in the sand after that, pulled me over to him. His flannel shirt smelled like Daddy used to after he cut the grass. I love that smell. Darrell hummed into my hair like he was singing a chorus over and over. I collapsed into him and cried like a baby. I think he was singing to both of us. On the drive over he said that the only time he felt alive was when he was singing, all he ever wanted was for someone to love his songs. 'It's okay, he sang, sometimes places we love, love us back, baby.' Beauty longs for us too.

"He skipped it like a stone across the lake. And that was it."

Four

Great-uncle Frank, a smug little bald fella, took pride in beating the crowd back to the house. After the funeral I wish I'd snapped his picture there in the front yard bounce-rocking in one of the clam-shaped lawn chairs whitewashed with bird doo. I'd a framed him between the two decorative wrought-iron posts seemingly holding up the front porch, or else moved him between Daddy's manicured boxwoods lining either side of the concrete walkway, the lime green hosepipe coiled on the ground beside the bushes. Either way, he was a sight sitting there pushing his false teeth in and out of his mouth with his tongue.

"Look a here, look a here . . . You must've come the long way," he teased as I passed him going up the front steps.

Inside, Momma was yelling into the phone, giving directions to the out-of-towners like her call was, literally, long-distance.

"Dogleg left a mile after the traffic light . . . You'll see a big gray fire tower . . . can't miss it . . . What? . . . No, I said one mile . . . That's right . . . A man crashed through the brick wall there at the corner . . . shook the glass from his hair and walked away . . . it's a light rose brick house with white shutters . . . Be careful . . . Yes . . . See you soon."

Soon the den was thick with relatives. And hot. Momma threw the windows open and cut on two box fans angled toward each other from opposite corners of the room. The sound of Uncle Billy's voice reminded me of rocks in a tumbler underground.

"I don't care what you say, if that bull gets mad, your ass is grass."

Over in the cramped kitchen, casseroles and deviled eggs lined copper-speckled counters, enough food to feed Daddy's extended family—every one of them a born eater.

Aunt Edna unveiled her famous buttermilk pie from beneath a red-and-white-checkered dishtowel, steam curling off the crust. She had a magician's "ta-da" look on her face. Her upturned palms gestured toward the pie as she slowly inched back away from the counter. Nobody paid her any mind, so she did it again.

"New hairdo, Aunt Edna?" I asked and she nodded. She sported what we referred to at barber school as "the Catholic nun," a home job with quarter-inch bangs, beginning to gray, cut straight and high across her forehead. Redundant, but it had the appeal of calling to mind the look and the demeanor of those who wore it.

After Uncle Billy accepted a sliver of her pie, "Sister" Edna lumbered out the front door hollering, "Come help me, Penny Sue." It took her a while to rearrange the junk piled in the trunk of her two-toned Pacer. Aunt Edna sold off overstock lamps and end tables from Daddy's furniture store out at the flea market every weekend to supplement her disability check. Now that he'd retired her stock was running low.

Splotchy-faced, breathing heavily, and falling from foot to foot, we lugged her accordion back inside the front door by the black leather handle. The bulky instrument caught the edge of Momma's rug and folded it in half as Edna struggled to situate the squeeze-box in the middle of the living room. Momma cut her eyes at me and whispered, "Poor thing. She's doing the best she can."

After pushing up the sleeves on her jack-o'-lantern sweatshirt and rubbing her hands together under the faucet, Momma reached up in the kitchen cabinet for her prescription bottle of "relaxation pills," then threw her pinhead back to wash one down with iced tea. Pink lipstick smudged the rim of dimpled glass. (Her lips rarely touched a glass unless she was in her own kitchen, for fear of filth.) After she swallowed, her lips drew up into a tight pink-looking pucker.

"Umm-ummm," she said under her breath like she always did when Daddy's family got under her skin.

❧

Daddy's side of the family planned to go all out to make sure Jebo's final request was honored. She'd always said, "Don't sit around 'sulled up' when I die; pitch a party when I'm gone."

Some of us were taking this request more seriously than others. In Jebo's honor, Aunt Edna set off the first two packs of bottle rockets out of an empty Dr Pepper bottle in the back-yard. One of the rockets caught Doc, the neighbor's German shepherd, broadside. Next, my first cousin Raymond Hewitt rode his Harley right up to the house. He carried a little step-stool, which he offered for the less-ambulatory relatives. If they could get on, he'd ride them up and down the access ramp built for Jebo in front of the house. Jebo used to love to fling her leg across the motorcycle and ride out in the country behind Raymond on Sunday afternoons.

All the fun came to a screeching halt after they found some of the younger kids playing hide-and-seek in that old turquoise refrigerator out in the garage. I swear, if Aunt Edna hadn't been taking those Bomb Pops popsicles out to them, every one of 'em would have suffocated.

~

Beads of sweat dotted Daddy's forehead when he finally burst through the front door after the reading of Jebo's will. An orange maple leaf stuck to his shoe. His turkey neck doubled over the tight collar of his stiff white shirt.

He found me sitting next to Uncle Billy on a metal folding chair somebody'd brought over from the church. Usually in the cramped den there was a blue sectional sofa and an orange-checkered love seat, plus two overstuffed chairs in that same muted weave as Daddy's recliner, not to mention an entertainment center it had taken Daddy two days to assemble up against the wall, and an octagonal coffee table so close to the couch you always bumped your shin.

Daddy'd cleared it out for this gathering so the room was less crowded with furniture, but it nearly tumped over from all the family leaning up against the wall.

"Get you a Pepsi, Porter," was Momma's greeting. She pointed to the Styrofoam cooler. He twisted off the top then jerk-signaled with the cold drink for me to follow him back out on the porch. His hair was styled for the funeral in a Porter Wagoner pompadour. His Grecian Formula, wearing off in patches, gave him a checkerboard hair pattern.

"Your daddy needs to get off his feet. He'll have himself a heart attack if he's not careful," Momma said as he and I walked out into the night.

"Who pulled your chain, May Dean?" Daddy shouted back. He grinned at Momma but dismissed her comment like he always did. I think that's how they stayed married.

Out on the porch, Daddy cracked his knuckles against the bottle. Above his head a moth banged into the porch light, its paper-thin wings distorted through Daddy's bottle when he tipped it up to take a swig. Behind him on the swing sat a brown paper bag from the A&P grocery store.

"What's that?" I asked.

"Jebo left these for you."

He reached around behind him and pulled out a bone-colored pocketbook that Jebo had always guarded like a family fortune, along with a Red Goose shoebox.

I froze.

"Go on, take 'em, Penny Sue. They're yours. Jebo underlined

it in her will: 'Make damn sure Penny Sue gets the Red Goose shoebox and my purse.'"

A sly grin broke across his face. "No telling what's in the box. You know your Jebo was a pistol."

Then he spoke to the night sky more than me. "Boy, I sure am glad she didn't suffer too long."

"Yes, sir."

"We're sure gonna miss her."

"Yes, sir."

"Hope you and your momma can find a way to make up, Penny Sue."

"I'm not even sure what we're fighting about."

"Your momma's real glad you're here, though she won't say it."

Daddy swept a spider off the porch with the toe of his dress loafer without killing it before he spoke again. He nodded to the items in his hand.

"I believe Jebo'd rise up outta that grave like Lazarus if they went to anyone else."

"Yes, sir."

Daddy tried to suck in his big stomach. "It's funny. All she left me was that push lawn mower and sledgehammer," he teased.

It was no secret that Jebo had favored me. Said I was a girl after her own heart. Momma hated it when Jebo said that.

"Something else I been meaning to say since you came home, Penny Sue. I'm worried about you."

"Daddy, I'm fine."

"You making enough to get by?" he asked, reaching for his wallet in his back pocket. "I want you to buy yourself something new to wear."

"Daddy, I told you, I'm fine."

Daddy pressed a bill into my hand and closed my fingers around it. "There you go, girl; it's all yours." He pinched my side playfully like he did when I was little, then cleared his throat and clapped his hands together to end our conversation. I didn't look at how much money it was until later.

I would have torn into the box right then if it hadn't been for the dull gray duct tape wrapped like a death grip end to end. I'd left my good haircutting scissors back in my kitchenette over in Memphis.

"Let me get back in here and reassure your momma. And listen, will you tell Billy to do something about those sideburns? He'll listen to you."

"All right."

"Don't stay out here too long by yourself, it's getting cold."

I winced when the storm door caught Daddy upside the nose when he threw it open.

"I'm all right. I'm fine," he said, waving me aside with one hand and covering the nick in his nose with the other.

I lurched toward the door, hooked the handle with my pointer finger, threw it back open long enough to work my way back into the house. The storm door slapped shut like a popgun, startling Aunt Edna out of half a cup of hot

26

chocolate. Luckily the liquid didn't scald her but only made a dark splatter spot on Momma's hardwood floor. Edna quickly took out a huge wad of powder blue Kleenex that was stuffed into the front pocket of her black pantsuit. She drew little circles with her foot to wipe up the mess. Never missed a beat, kept right on talking to anybody who'd listen, spewing crumbs of walnut brownie from her mouth on the "P" words.

"Penny Sue, I'm prepared to sing something when you are."

"In a minute," I answered.

"Please!"

"I said in a minute."

I had to check on Momma. She'd been known to "over-pill" herself in stressful situations. And Daddy's family rattled her. I was afraid she might pull one of her stunts. Last time we all got together for Daddy's birthday, she got "overstimulated" and locked herself in the hall closet. "Has anybody seen Momma?"

Then I spotted her standing beneath the cuckoo clock, gnawing her nails to the nub, spitting white bits into the Tennessee walking horse trash can on the floor beside her.

"Stirring trouble from the grave," was her comment intended for my ears only.

I changed the subject. "Momma, you want a plate of food?"

"I guess," she answered.

Around the corner, leaning against the kitchen counter, Uncle Billy was telling his tired joke about the priest, the rabbi, and the Bengal tiger; punctuating his tiger remarks with two hooked fingers on the sides of his headlike ears. That dark suit, along with the fat knot in his sea-green tie, made him look vulnerable. I was used to seeing Uncle Billy in overalls and work boots. Never seen his straggly hair glued down like that in a comb-over style.

All the while Momma, pocketbook pinned to her side, kept a running commentary on Daddy's family whenever she could get my attention.

"They say that *my* side of the family is nuts. Look at them." Momma wore that phrase out over the years.

"Did you see this?" I held up the purse and Red Goose shoebox.

"I saw it," Momma said. "That's why I said she's trying to stir some trouble from the grave."

Her hand cupped a curl near the nape of her neck and lifted it. "No telling *what* she put inside that box."

"Momma. Stop it. Why did you hate Jebo?"

"I didn't hate her. And keep your voice down. I *disliked* her."

"What in the world did she ever do to you?"

I set a plate of fried chicken and green bean casserole on the counter in front of her with a navy napkin. Momma picked up a plastic fork, stabbed a bite of casserole, and blurted, "For one thing, Jebo begged your daddy not to marry me. Told him I wasn't marriage material."

Everything about my momma—her mouth, her thinning overpermed hair, the narrow stripes of her penciled eyebrows, even her gangly limbs—was drawn inward toward some invisible bunker where she holed up and protected herself from imagined enemies.

"You're exaggerating. That was years ago, Momma," I reminded her.

"I'll never forget it. Ever."

Five

Jebo's bedroom was the first door on the left. It was unrecognizable now. Momma'd hired a cleaning woman from the Ladies Auxiliary. They'd dusted and vacuumed Jebo clean from the room. All that lingered was a pinched antiseptic smell of Pine-Sol and mothballs; the odor made my tooth fillings tingle. Before she died, Jebo's room had been a happy wreck; housedresses, underwear, and thin white socks were usually flung over her wicker rocking chair, mismatched shoes shoved up under the bed, every now and then a crumpled Baby Ruth wrapper was left on top of her chest of drawers; now, it was neat as a pin. Her clothes were hung perfectly and lifelessly in the cedar closet, each shoe matched with its twin, the pairs pointing in the same direction.

On top of Jebo's dresser were three remnants of her peculiar personality: a small rectangular tape recorder for song lyrics she'd written, two unopened packages of bottle rockets, and a tambourine with long red-ribbon streamers that she played at birthday celebrations. I'd never noticed all the knotholes in the dark brown paneling in Jebo's room before. The imperfections in the wood looked like scary open-mouthed faces.

I eased into the white wicker rocking chair beside the stacked single beds.

"Open the box, Penny Sue." I wasn't sure if the voice was Jebo's or my own.

The nightstand drawer held a Swiss Army knife I'd given to Jebo for a birthday present. She'd specifically requested regulation size with the can-opener feature, just in case we ever went car camping. We never did. The red knife was on top of her clipped collection of magazine articles about Liberace.

"Liberace is the most talented man on the face of the earth," she'd say. "You can tell he's successful by the way he carries himself onstage." I opened the widest blade and slid it up under the gray duct tape on the shoebox and worked open the lid.

Right off I recognized the black leather: soft and worn, about the size of a five-by-seven picture frame. I ran a trembling finger along the tattered spine of the book on the top of the stack.

"What in the world?"

But of course I knew Jebo had kept all these books protectively tucked away on the wall side of the beds ever since I could remember. No one, and I mean no one, was ever allowed to step foot over on that back side near her books.

One by one, I lifted each diary out of the shoebox. I might as well have been lifting a fragile robin's egg out of its nest the way I ran my fingers up under each book and reverently laid it on her nubby white-cotton bedspread. Maybe, like a good pair of shoes, these leather books would guide me to someplace new off my current path of self-destruction. On the outside of the top volume, she'd stuck a yellow Post-it note. Written in blue Magic Marker was "#1." The book beneath the first diary was identical, black worn leather, except for the yellow "#2" stuck to the cover. After lifting out "#3," the box was empty. I scratched the bottom of the cardboard box, trying to produce what I wanted to magically appear. Nothing. Nothing on the floor either.

"Where's number four?"

Jebo made a point over the years to let me know these diaries were a set of four books, never to be divided. I recall, almost word for word, a conversation she'd instigated last Christmas. Jebo was a teetotaler who loved a good margarita. Liquor was not allowed in the house except for the "flavoring" she kept in a decanter to pour on top of homemade boiled custard on holidays. She'd turned to me that evening with a good deal of "flavorin'" on her breath and whispered loudly, "Secret treasures sit in that diary, Penny Sue. When I die, read all four and don't skip a word." For a second an unusual tone crept into her voice, honest like the sound of a banjo. She softened me, got up under the armor I usually wore over my heart.

"One day you're gonna find your way, sugar. Everything will just fall into place."

The moment didn't last long before Jebo playfully winked one eye so hard it pulled up the same side corner of her mouth. Quickly she changed the subject.

Sitting there on the chair, I clutched book #1 and felt the hot sting of tears. Over the past few years I'd stayed away from Jebo; especially after the DUI charge, she was too hard to hide from. She had my number.

I opened the front flap of the leather diary; the paper was creamy and soft around the edges. Her name, Loreen Elizabeth Pritchett, was written in black ink in the right-hand corner of the page. A piece of notebook paper folded in thirds was taped to the first blank page.

October 1, 1989
Dear Penny Sue,

I figure I've got about two weeks to live. I want to write this down, while I still got the strength to pick up a pencil. I wish we were sitting face-to-face but I'm stuck in this bed and you're haircutting over in Memphis so this will have to do. There are some things I should have told you before now. Your momma made me promise I wouldn't while I still had breath in my body. If you're reading this letter, I've drawn my last. I'm leaving you my diaries so you'll know the truth. There's too much in there to wade through all of it. I've underlined what I think are the important entries. Read them slow, let it all sink in for a while. I pray I'm doing the right thing here.

I'm going to close this letter now. I know you must have so many questions. You were always a child after my own heart. I hope I get to give these to you myself, but if I don't Porter will.

I love you,
Jebo

Deep creases in the letter made me think she'd folded and refolded it several times, so much that it remembered its shape as I kissed it and taped it back onto the book. The open mouths locked in the pine paneling strained to speak out of their eerie silence. Then I heard the first guitar chord ringing out in the room. This time it was Hank Williams. He was singing, "I'm So Lonesome I Could Cry." I knew the radio was turned off. I sat on the side of the bed, swaying back and forth to the slow rhythm in my head before I turned the page.

I didn't have to go far in the first book to find several passages underlined with a yellow highlighter. The underlined passages were written in black ink, the others in blue. Jebo had carefully rewritten the underlined passages for me.

June 1, 1960 — Raining cats and dogs. Loretta Lynn's singing "I'm a Honky Tonk Girl" on the radio. Porter finally drug that girl he's seeing over here. Cute as a bug, but shy. She's from way off over near Hickory, NC. He met her on a furniture-buying trip. I was playing and singing Hank Williams when they walked in. Embarrassed Porter to death. She calls herself May Dean Maples. No connection to the wealthy Maples over there. Told Porter she's eighteen. I hope she's not lying about her age like I did. At least she's not pregnant like I was. Invited them to go with me to the rock quarry Sunday week. I think we'll picnic and swim.

June 5, 1960 — Sunny, high 85 today. Cloudy. Edna got a new job making beds at the Howard Johnson's. I hope she keeps it. Out at the farm last night Billy's bay mare colicked—walked her till dawn. Said the bull was acting up too. Porter, May Dean, and I went swimming on Sunday. Girl didn't even own a swimsuit, borrowed one of mine. It hung off of her. She talked a blue streak while Porter swung off the rope. (Sometimes he still acts like a little boy.) I mean poured her heart out. Maples family's troubled—no doubt about it. May Dean's momma died when she was 13, May Dean helped raise them two little sisters. Dixie and Kate—I think. Her daddy drank like a fish. He beat all three of those little girls black and blue when he got tooted. Must have done it pretty regular from the way she was squalling. Seems everybody in Hickory knew about it. She was real ashamed of her situation.

June 13, 1961—Got into the low 90s today. Porter stormed over here mad as a hornet. Whooping and hollering. May Dean lied to him. Told him I said they shouldn't get married. I said no such a thing. May Dean overheard me talking to Edna about her father the other night. All I said was that Frank Maples might be stumbling drunk when he walked her down the aisle. It's the plain truth. Porter better calm her butt down.

June 14, 1961—Hot and muggy. Can't get Patsy Cline's "I Fall to Pieces" out of my head. Patsy was injured today in a car crash. Porter and May Dean tied the knot yesterday. Billy stood up proud as punch as best man—he'd outgrown *that suit. Edna's shoes pinched her feet, but I told her she's lucky to be a bridesmaid for the first time. I sang "How Great Thou Art" at the reception—a cappella. Not a one of May Dean's kinfolks came over to the wedding. Might call over there and give them a piece of my mind. Fellowship hall was burning up. My new daughter-in-law fainted and fell over on Edna after her part of the vows—nerves. Luna had some Valium tucked in her pocketbook. She calmed right down after that. Nice service.*

Momma would lose her mind if she knew Jebo had left this information for me. After reading the first few entries, I was more scared than anything else.

Six

"Penny Sue. Penny! Phone's for you," Momma hollered up the stairs. I slammed the diary shut and stuffed it way up under the white dust ruffle on the bottom bunk along with the shoebox and purse. Down at the bottom of the steps Momma had the receiver trapped in her bosom. "Sounds like that hairdresser boss of yours over in Memphis," she said, furrowing her brow. "He sure talks funny."

The white spiral cord, bunched and tangled, wouldn't stretch all the way back to Jebo's room, so I plopped down on the stairs and shooed Momma away.

"Hello."

"Penny Sue, Doris got head burn from the perm chemicals you left on her hair. We might have a lawsuit on our hands." Boyd always exaggerated.

"Sorry, Boyd. My grandmother was dying. In fact, she died."

Boyd Pitts was a Yankee transplant who learned to cut hair in the army. He made a living wooing women. A silver fox if there ever was one. Boyd hired me right out of barber college to work part-time at his two-chair operation out back of his house in a prefab storage shed fortified with electricity. Women loved Boyd because he entertained them with silly card tricks and off-color jokes while they waited up under the dryer.

"I'm sorry to hear that, but you can't just walk off like that. Doris was real upset. You know she's got heart trouble."

I didn't believe him but kept on listening.

"One other thing, smarty-pants . . . um . . . after you left, your parole officer called."

I cupped my hand over the receiver. "That's enough, Boyd. I know you're lying now. I finished parole six months ago."

"Well, one thing's for sure, you're slacking around here and I'm about to send you packing. I could rent your chair out tomorrow, Penny Sue."

"C'mon, Boyd. Give me a break, okay? My husband left me, my grandmother just died . . ." I could see him fluffing his hair in the mirror, the phone trapped between his shoulder and ear, Christmas lights he left up year-round flashing.

"Why should I?" I'm sure he was pouting into the mirror.

"I'm going to have to call you back later."

"I'm dead serious, Penny Sue. I can't have this."

"Bye, Boyd." I heard him still talking as I hung up.

❧

The funeral crowd was still milling around the kitchen counter picking at the food when the six o'clock news came on. My first cousin, Raymond Hewitt Pritchett, wore a thick brown braid down the middle of his back and waxed his handlebar mustache to perfection. That night Raymond had ants in his pants. He kept hopping up and down off the couch to switch channels on the console television he'd angled toward him. Said he didn't want to miss the weather forecast on Channel 5.

Momma must have seen me searching the couch cushions for my car keys.

"It's getting too late, Penny Sue. Don't drive back to Memphis."

And then, before I could answer, she switched subjects. "Why pants at the funeral? Pants?! Everybody saw."

"I'm grown. I can wear what I want to."

"You wore them just to spite me, didn't you?"

Momma didn't have the presence of mind to realize that although I'd kept a blond Samsonite suitcase packed in the back of my Chevette ever since Darrell and I started having trouble, funeral attire wasn't part of my packing. I only had essentials: a pair of jeans, two clean pink T-shirts, underwear, and my favorite purple toothbrush that I'd used so long the bristles lay horizontal.

"Momma . . . ," I began, but I let it go.

Raymond Hewitt yanked his mouth over to one side, talking away from the television, eyes still on the screen. "Don't push her, Penny Sue. I'm not sure I'm up for seeing your momma blow a gasket." Raymond was Jebo's grand-nephew. He didn't spend near as much time with her growing up as I did because he lived over in Little Rock. His voice was laid-back, slightly lazy; it cracked every so often as if he was getting hoarse.

"Remember that time Jebo wrecked into the pecan tree?"

"Sure I do. Two front-row tickets to the Grand Ole Opry."

"Wasn't Patsy Cline supposed to perform that night?"

"No, Loretta Lynn. What were we—about twelve years old?"

"I'm five years your senior so I was close to seventeen." Raymond finally turned away from the TV and faced me, mindlessly twisting the end of his mustache.

"Now that was a night to remember. Jebo and I packed enough Polaroid film to snap instant pictures of every Roy Acuff, Porter Wagoner, and Minnie Pearl that stepped up on that stage. We planned to arrange the pictures alphabetically in an album once we got back home."

"Yeah, I remember Jebo getting all dolled up that night." The crow's-feet around his eyes deepened as he smiled.

"You're right, Raymond. Jebo wore that fancy black jacket—rhinestones sewn in daisy patterns all across the shoulders. She looked sharp, except for the double pair of glasses. Remember how she'd stack a pair of wraparound sunglasses on top of her prescription lenses?"

"I don't quite remember that little detail. How did she hit that tree?" Raymond had all but forgotten about the newscast.

"Backing down the drive, Jebo's foot slipped and hit the gas pedal instead of the brake. I can vouch for the fact that there was no drinking involved. She rammed the pecan tree so hard it killed it."

"I'd keep my voices down if I were y'all," Raymond's older brother Hubert whispered, passing by on his way to the kitchen, that empty sleeve where the arm oughtta be swinging.

"I know for sure that May Dean don't like no loose-lippin' going on in her house."

Raymond dropped the volume a hair. "I was inside with your momma watching it happen from the window. May Dean clutched her curls, pitched a fit."

"Did you know I hit my head on the dashboard?"

"Hmm," he replied. "You'd a thought Jebo committed manslaughter the way your momma barreled out the front door like a house afire. She beat on the car hood with her fist so hard it made a huge dent as I recall. That woman snapped."

"Do you remember what she said when she came back in the house?"

"Remind me." Raymond was clearly enjoying himself.

"'Don't you two tell anybody about what just happened out there; it's family business. Emphasis on the word *family*. Don't breathe a word.' She didn't seem to care one bit about the giant bump on my head."

Seven

Pouring myself a cup of decaf, I decided Momma was right about one thing: it was too late to drive back to Memphis. Aunt Edna flopped down on the couch beside me. "Where's that husband of yours tonight, Penny Sue?"

"Um . . . well, I'm not exactly sure, Aunt Edna."

Momma had told me not to tell Aunt Edna that Darrell left me. Said it might affect her negatively—whatever that was supposed to mean. The thought of Darrell right now made my stomach churn. I thought of how, if Jebo were alive, she'd defy Momma and answer Aunt Edna for me. On top of that, she'd embellish a little like she always did:

"Darrell's not much to look at," she'd say. "A stocky fella, five foot six inches tall in his steel-toe work boots. But, he has *huge* biceps. They call him Popeye over at the gym." Jebo would raise her eyebrows in a suggestive way.

"Evidently, Betsy Burnett, that underfed Irish setter–looking gal behind the counter at the Jim Dandy Market, took a shine to those muscles too. Poor thing . . . rail thin. Penny Sue called that haircut of hers a 'David Partridge,' didn't you, Penny Sue?"

"Yes, ma'am," I'd reply.

Then she'd continue. "Betsy could have licked salt off the top of Darrell's head standing sock-footed." I imagine Jebo taking a long drag off her cigarette right at that point in the story. Then on a big exhale she'd say sarcastically, "Poor Darrell. The whole mess was on account of that Polaroid of him with that prizewinning bass. The picture conveniently fell out of his shirt pocket onto the floor in front of Betsy. 'Why did he have to lean down so far you ask?'" her question intended to entice her listeners, "Well, I just so happen to know—because Darrell told me himself—that the picture slipped out when he leaned down to grab a pouch of Red Man off the bottom shelf, further staining his brown teeth, I might add."

Jebo would point at her listeners like she was presenting evidence to a jury. "You and I both know Red Man don't sit on the bottom shelf at the Jim Dandy—it's up by the register. Yeah, Betsy couldn't control herself. Darrell claims his arm was flexed in the photo because the fish weighed so much. Penny Sue and I saw that same photo, didn't we, shug?"

Like her straight man, I'd answer, "Yes, ma'am, with our own two eyes."

"We weren't impressed, were we?"

"No, ma'am."

"We thought he needed a good shower and shave, didn't we, hon?"

"You are right about that, Jebo."

She'd wrap up with Darrell's exact words: "Betsy was fairly impressed with everything she saw," then finish with "Long story short, 'Popeye' and Betsy are now shacked up with her three kids in a two-bedroom over off the interstate."

I couldn't get enough distance to tell it like Jebo. So when Aunt Edna grew bored with my silence, she just went back for seconds on the pie.

Eight

It irritated Momma that Stella Prine rang the doorbell when the storm door was already standing open.

"It's wide open," Momma yelled in the door's direction.

Stella, the next-door neighbor, was a gap-toothed, squat woman with a platinum wig. She maneuvered her lumpy hips through the doorway carrying a cast-iron pot.

"Hi, May Dean. Hope I'm not too late. How's everybody? I brought you some October beans," she said, trying to ignore Aunt Edna, who was flapping her arms, pretending to fly off the back of the couch. She'd safety-pinned two corners of a baby blue bath towel around her neck to make a Wonder Woman cape.

Stella was the one who told Momma about Darrell and Betsy. I hadn't seen Stella since I moved to Memphis seven years ago, but I'd never forget the sound of her voice as long as I lived. Jebo could imitate her perfectly. One day after work I called to commiserate with Jebo: she'd gotten sick, and Darrell had left me. I asked Jebo to reenact the telephone call for me, just to satisfy my dark sense of humor. She agreed:

"Good morning. Y'all doing all right?" Jebo had the nasal whine down pat.

"I hate to tell you this, but I have bad news. This weekend I saw Penny Sue's husband out on Pickwick Lake with some other woman."

I knew that Jebo would make a pretend telephone of her thumb and pinkie finger and hold it up to her ear like she was Stella.

"I was minding my own business, tying flies, casting off the pontoon when Darrell and some little bitty redhead whizzed by the boat." Jebo embellished the story at this point and said that Stella jumped up out of her deck chair so fast she ripped a hole in the seat of her swimsuit, the high-piled Dolly Parton wig she wore going ever-which-a-way. Then Jebo fell right back into Stella's voice.

"Darrell and Redhead were stacked right on top of one another, inner-tubing behind a MasterCraft." I could hear Momma screaming in the background at Jebo, hollering for her to stop telling the story. She didn't want to hear it ever again. Momma hated our family being the butt end of town gossip worse than she hated my heart getting broken.

Unable to stomach Stella, I barreled out of the kitchen heading up to Jebo's room through the crowd. Made it to the foot of the narrow stairway before looking back over my shoulder. Daddy had already spooned an obligatory lump of her beans onto his flimsy paper plate. The sea of kinfolks was dizzying. I felt like I'd tried to please most every one of them, especially my momma, all my life. And for what?

"Penny Sue, you left your plate a food on the counter," I heard Momma saying.

For a minute—old men and women, children, siblings and distant cousins, gestured to one another in slow motion. Clunky movements, not a graceful one among us. That's when the sound track came on in my head for the third time, midsong, blotting out the choir of conversations. This time the tune was the Statler Brothers' "Flowers on the Wall," a song that Jebo loved to sing.

Country music was like connective tissue between Jebo and me. It created a pathway into the world of feelings, a world I otherwise tried to avoid. When Jebo played a new song to me, I could—how do I put this?—I could make sense of the weight on my chest. Most of the time *lost* was the only thing I felt. When I asked Jebo how she dealt with things that happened to her, she'd say, "You do what you gotta do, Penny Sue." Jebo wouldn't say much about the things that bothered her. Her answer was to hold up that spiral notebook she tied to her belt and shake it in the air.

~

I'd turned back to sprint up the stairs, that full plate of food untouched, when I heard Aunt Edna, her mouth full of thigh meat now, hollering, "Nobody'll sing with me!"

"Sorry, Aunt Edna," I answered her. "Ask Sheila; she loves to sing."

"Sheila don't know the songs."

"Well, find somebody else."

I spun back around and slung her a miniature box of Milk Duds from a cut-glass bowl holding Momma's Halloween candy. Edna shook her head from side to side, but she never refused candy. I escaped up the stairs. At the top I heard her voice asking Daddy and Uncle Billy to sing "Onward, Christian Soldiers" with her. And soon they were singing a cappella.

One time I asked Momma what exactly was wrong with Aunt Edna, but she wouldn't give me a straight answer. Nothing I could sink my teeth into. Epilepsy was mentioned, or possibly a mild form of lead poisoning as a child.

Aunt Edna played accordion about like she looked out on the world, half-assed. Literally, one lens of her large glasses was medicinally frosted, hiding the dark hazel of her left eye. That mysterious eye curled up behind the lens like a lazy housecat. Growing up I wondered aloud what it was like to look out on the world with just one eye, but Momma wouldn't let me ask Aunt Edna. Lens prescriptions were very personal, according to her. One Saturday night Aunt Edna fell asleep at our house watching *Lawrence Welk*. I carefully picked up the gold frames off the coffee table, slipped them onto my face, and turned toward the window. Through the clear lens I saw fuzzy leaves on the trees. The eye restrained by the frosted fence saw a white haze and caused my vision to bounce back onto itself. Maybe that's what it was like to be Aunt Edna. Half-trapped or half-unoccupied. When Aunt Edna gave a short snort and turned onto her side, I quickly replaced the glasses on the coffee table. She snored on.

Nine

Finally safe in the sanctity of Jebo's room, my mind whirred at the thought of what those diaries held for me. More than anybody, Jebo'd been witness to my life growing up. I hungered now for her view of it all—of me. I scanned the pages, looking for my birthday. There it was: November 15, 1963.

November 15, 1963—Frost last night. Baby girl came a week early—everything's fine. Penny Sue Pritchett— pretty as a picture. Bald-headed and pale blue eyes. May Dean's dead-dog tired. They cut her open to take the baby. It'll take her a while to recover from that. Can't help but think of Edna again. If we'd gotten her to the doctor in time, they might have been able to get the fever down.

Jebo's narrative loosened up something tight in my chest— a reprieve from the stifling tension downstairs. I sped ahead to the next entry.

Now, Jebo's penmanship was something special. She and I had swapped letters back and forth during my first and final semester at Ross's Barber College in Memphis. In the letters,

Jebo's left-handed cursive slanted so far to the right that it nearly touched the lines on the notebook paper, like chickens leaning down to peck at the ground. About every third or fourth word was legible; the rest I had to piece together like a jigsaw puzzle.

But that was years ago. I was out of practice. Deciphering her chicken scratch was proving to be a challenge. What I didn't expect in a million years was the way those slanted words began to splash all over the page.

One here, one there. Some lines were short, others long. There were extra spaces in between words in the same sentence.

Had Jebo been slowly losing her mind?

"What the hell?"

Then it dawned on me.

Slowly it sank in . . . Some of the entries were poems. My Jebo had written poetry.

The green spiral notebook she tied with a kite string to the belt loop of her housedress came to mind. Every time Jebo began taking notes in her little book, Momma got a white ring around her mouth like she was going to throw up. A lot of time Jebo'd write things down after she and Momma disagreed. Somehow I'd always thought she was keeping score and that someday there'd be an endgame and someone would call a winner. I think it helped Jebo mind her temper.

I worked to control my breathing. It hissed as I blew it out through the straw of my lips. Outside the window, a crescent moon mocked me with a thin smile. I read each line slowly.

Fill Her Up

Midnight, outside Memphis,
the only light for miles.
An eighteen-wheeler runs over a rubber hose
(the ding so loud we dance
in the gas station office).

Momma collects herself for customers:
tugs her 3-hook bra,
shoves her hair
under a Tommy's Esso ball cap,

The name Ethel cross-stitched
on her station shirt
like she's become
one of the ingredients
in the gas she pumps
to put me through school.

She lingers longer than I'd like
into driver-side windows.
Young men cling to her cleavage.
Nasty answers to her question,
"Fill 'er up?"

Car after Cadillac car,
she rams the shiny shaft

of the jointed nozzle
down the dark hole of the tanks.
Knocking her knuckle on the back window
let's them know she's through.

An oil-stained rag hangs off her pocket.
Around her neck she wears a locket,
a picture of me pressed inside.

I've seen her pull out prematurely,
watched the fuel puddle,
drip down the drain
as she strikes a match on her zipper,
to light another smoke.

Lord knows that woman plays with fire.

For years I burn
with what I learn there
on the outskirts of Memphis—
a young girl can't fathom
what a hard woman knows.

*The memory hit me like a ton of bricks. I see her clear as day. Fannie
Ferrell's momma, Linda, cookin' chicken and dumplin's at the stove
wearing filthy blue coveralls. Fannie's brother accidentally shot her
in the arm while messing with the safety on the shotgun. She had to
quit work at State Farm after that and take a night-shift job at the*

Esso station. Fannie and I were jumping rope in the garage when the ambulance arrived. Momma never let me spend the night over there again. Said Linda Ferrell'd gotten trashy. Jebo went by to see her every once in a while.

⌐

Crickets screamed in the dark. I got my bearings by navigating the "stars" overhead. Loretta Lynn, Roy Acuff, and Minnie Pearl, diamonds in a federal bunk-bed sky, twinkled above me. Slowly my hands recognized what I'd clutched as I slept. Jebo's poems. "A young girl can't fathom what a hard woman knows. A young girl can't fathom . . ."

The grandfather clock boomed three times. Time enough to finish one diary before daylight. Six or seven entries deep I screeched to a stop.

Guest Preacher at Prayer Meeting

He swaggers, reeking Jack Daniel's
into the microphone.
The bulbous mesh microphone
divides our living room/den:
those who are, those who aren't.
"Christians, adorn yourselves with Chr-eye-st,"
he exhorts through capped teeth.
Wearing all white:
double-knit suit,

wide-collar shirt,
alabaster platform shoes.

Enraptured, we gawk, widemouthed
like the bass we just deep-fried for supper.
Playing on his line:
"Oh sinner, come home."
Sister Nell acquiesces.
Walks the makeshift aisle—
metal chairs lined in three short rows.
Bears the cross she wears around her neck to him.

James 4:12 stumbles to welcome,
writes Nell's name into a black book,
shouts, "God won't forsake those listed here."
Piano hymns swell, the air seductive.

"James" runs diamond cluster hands through coal-black
   hair.
Denounces the evils of liquor-by-the-drink,
cocks his head to heaven, listening to dark angels urging
   climax.
Driving divine words down the backs of our throats.

I don't know if anybody
truly came to know the Lord that night.

Later that summer I did hear tell
Aunt Nell came to *know*
the guest preacher at the prayer meeting.

*How could I forget? Mid-August. Muggy heat. Record temperatures
hovered near 100 for two weeks straight. We hosted the Summer Home
Revival service. I pulled Momma into the hall closet to get away from
the crowd. She had big sweat rings under her arms.*

"What's the matter with you, Penny Sue?"

*"That man makes my stomach hurt, Momma. He stared at me
all during dinner. Said I had pretty hair."*

"Lower your voice, Penny Sue."

"He asked if he could have a bite of my corn on the cob."

*"You're making things up, young lady. Now, get back in there
and help with the dinner dishes. Your cousins can't do all the work."*

"Something's wrong with that man, Momma. I can feel it."

*"Don't you say another word." She put her hand over my mouth.
"He's gonna baptize Aunt Katie Nell tomorrow night. You'll ruin her
special day."*

Jebo omitted, let's say, "tarnished parts" of our family his-
tory in her stories. Abrupt endings were common. I thought
she'd been holding back something. Maybe she feared that
we weren't prepared for the dark struggles of adult life. Had
she kept them all here waiting for just the right moment? Or
greedily tucked them away for her own pleasure?

Ten

Just as the sun was beginning to turn the sky on . . . like a quiet lamp, I woke and tiptoed to the bathroom. I could still detect the faint smell of smoke. This was Jebo's smoking sanctuary. No one was allowed in but me. She and I developed quite a ritual when I was little: Jebo would slip off to the bathroom shortly after supper. My signal was the hum sound of the exhaust fan. Roughly thirty seconds later I was supposed to approach the door and give three short knocks.

"What's the password?" she'd demand, her voice sounding like she was somewhere down in the bottom of the commode.

My head flat against the floor, I'd whisper, "Chateaubriand," under the door.

Sometimes she'd make me say it five times fast before she'd unlock the door. Jebo loved to hear that million-dollar word come out of my little mouth. Jebo and I never talked too much there in the cramped bathroom. Like a vicarious rebel, I sat silent with her in her secret spot. I'd climb up on the side of the pink porcelain sink while Jebo hunkered on the dark green bath mat draped over the side of the tub, forearms resting on her thighs, her back curled into a C shape.

Jebo smoked Camels; kept a pack hidden on the bottom shelf of the closet behind the towels and sheets. She also kept a box of Shoney's matches hidden in the cleavage inside her enormous bra. It was like we were reenacting some sort of ancient ceremony. I can still hear the *scritch* of the match as she let me strike it against the grout between the counter tiles, can feel the heat of the fire as I cupped my hand around the business end of her cigarette until it was good and lit. Then she'd offer me a puff, knowing I'd decline every time. While lit, it perched on her lip and bobbed up and down if she spoke. Since she rarely ashed, I'd stare, petrified; afraid the fire'd drop on her dress. Miraculously, at the last possible moment, she'd skillfully tap the droopy ash into the toilet water. It made a little sizzle.

When I heard Momma and Daddy stirring, I crept back to Jebo's room and slid back in bed. The soft pink of first light seeped through the ruffled white curtains. Pine-Sol and moth-balls still hung in the air.

Momma hooked her head around the door at seven o'clock sharp. "Penny Sue?"

I pretended I'd been asleep.

"There's coffee. Don't mind getting your own breakfast, do you? I can't get your daddy out the door, you know how slow he is." She rolled her eyes. "Don't mind the mess. I'll clean up when I get back. We've got to get on the road. I want to get a jump on the drive over to Arkansas."

"Come on, Porter," she hollered down the hall.

Momma trained Daddy to speak a language called "tight-lip," but he'd let it slip that Jebo had willed him ten acres over in Little Rock. Now that Jebo was gone, Momma was anxious to get rid of it, and the faster the better.

Retying a clear plastic rain hat securely beneath her chin, she turned back to me. "They're calling for rain. Make sure and roll up your car windows," Momma chirped.

"All right," I flatlined.

"We'll be home in a few days. Stay here as long as you like." She hesitated. "But only if you want to."

"Good-bye, Mother." I covered my head with the white pillow. She tried to maneuver her arms around the unwieldy lump of my body for a good-bye hug. I heard her red roller suitcase scrape the baseboards, then *bump bump* down the stairs.

"Make sure you lock the doors every time you leave," she called. Then I heard her turn the lock.

I didn't unclench my jaw until I heard the dull metal of the dead bolt slide into the door. Not five seconds later the slide *thud* came again. It was Daddy. He stuck his head back in and yelled, "Bye, sis. Take care of yourself, you hear me?" then lightly pulled the door shut again.

⌒

Measuring out Maxwell House into Momma's Mr. Coffee, I heard Charlie Pride's "Kiss an Angel Good Morning" playing in my head. I had no idea what caused my music to turn on and off. Then the phone bell pealed and I quick-walked down the hallway toward the phone. I caught my funny bone on the wall corner.

"Ow. What the hell?" Hearing my voice for the first time in the empty house startled me more than the sharp stab of pain.

By the time I got out "Hello," whoever'd called had hung up. Still cussing what was probably a condolence caller, I found my faded red Ross's Barber College sweatshirt in Jebo's bottom drawer and slipped it over my head.

The cane-bottom chair in the breakfast nook creaked beneath my weight as I began to flip through the Living section of the *Daily Courier*. Ironically, the Living section was where they cataloged the dead in Cheatham County. Jebo's obituary should be in there, but the only names I recognized were Wendell Golightly and my old piano teacher, Lynette Sams. Both buried yesterday. Wendell, a year ahead of me in high school, evidently died of an "extended illness." He'd played the shoulder–strap bass drum in our high school marching band. We had a date to the homecoming dance my senior year. I heard he had a psychotic breakdown. It must have slipped Momma's mind to tell me he died. Where was Jebo's obituary?

With my hot cup of coffee in one hand and a leftover ham and biscuit in the other, I walked barefoot outside to the mailbox, careful to favor my bandaged toe. The multicolored rooster Momma'd stencil-painted on the mailbox made me smile in spite of myself. When you raised the flag to signal a pickup, the little red part on top of his head stuck up. She thought it might keep squirrels away from the mailbox.

Inside the mailbox, Sears, Roebuck and JCPenney sale catalogs were rubber-banded around a thick stack of bills and condolence cards. Walking back to the house I hollered a drawn-out "Hellllloooo" and waved to Stella Prine next door, wearing red stretch pants beneath her housecoat and struggling with her morning toe touches in the front yard. A sign in her yard read "Diabetic socks for sale." Stella's front-yard flexibility had inspired Jebo to keep herself in shape all these years.

Back in the kitchen, I flipped through the stack of cards, recognizing several of the return addresses: 4227 Mt. Pleasant Drive, Little Rock, Arkansas—Aunt Jo and Uncle Bob; Rt. 5, Corinth, Mississippi, must have been Uncle Fonzie and Aunt Nezzalee. An oversized card from Hazen, Arkansas, had to be from that pack of second cousins. They love anything supersized.

The orange envelope stuck out like a sore thumb. A Halloween card? My full name, Penny Sue Pritchett, was typewritten across the front of the envelope. Whoever sent it stuck a specialty stamp of boxer Eddie Eagan upside down in the right-hand corner. I hadn't received any mail at this address for years. And there was no return address. I tore off the end of the envelope. Inside was a plain three by five white card on which *Reader's Digest* large-print words had been cut out and pasted. It read:

PENNY SUE,
WHAT'S NUMBER 4 WORTH TO
YOU?
IF YOU WANT THE dIARY
BACK—DO AS I SAY!
RECORd POEMS ONTO
CASSETTE
DO IT OR NEVER SEE NUMBEr
4 AGAIN

I flipped the note over from front to back, again and again. "Is this a joke? Who in the world would go to the trouble of sending something crazy like this?" Like I'd just caught a hundred-pound feed sack tossed off the back of a two-ton truck, I staggered to keep my balance beneath the weight. I wobbled back a couple of steps, then plopped into the chair at the kitchen table. Stared at fruit flies fighting over a brownish banana in a bowl.

I held the note to my nose and sniffed. Darrell'd been heavy-handed with his aftershave. If the note reeked of Old Spice, he'd be the most likely suspect. The card, however, smelled more like fried chicken.

Who in the world? I thought.

I quickly creased the note and shoved it into my tight front jeans pocket. Searched the room to get my bearings: aqua stove and refrigerator still there . . . okay; white pop-up toaster, check; *There'll be time for cleaning and cooking . . . children grow up when we're not looking* still cross-stitched and ironically hung on the wall beside the little pantry closet . . . so I guessed this wasn't a dream.

I shifted my eyes around the room to make sure I was all alone. Don't know how long I sat in that position. I do know my hands buzzed like they were going numb.

⁓

When my coffee kicked in, I grabbed a Hefty bag and lit out for the backyard to pick up the bottle rockets and trash from the get-together after the funeral. I hated for Momma and Daddy to come back to a big mess. As I worked, the note nagged in my pocket, the names of potential writers scrolling through my mind. Edna . . . Raymond . . . Darrell . . . Nobody seemed to fit. I hauled heavy plastic garbage bags to the road, moved the couch and chairs back in place, and rubbed the little rings left by Coke and Sprite bottles with a mixture of mayonnaise and cigarette ash. Jebo's own recipe.

Late that afternoon Momma called to say that the farm sale had hit a snag, and that it might be a week to ten days before they could get back. She wanted to know "would I stay at the house and keep an eye on things?"

"Momma?" I hesitated.

"What's wrong? Darrell hasn't contacted you, has he? He might come over if he thinks we're out of town."

"Settle down, I'm fine. It's just that . . . that, well." Suddenly, saying something about the ransom note felt silly.

"Aunt Jo and Uncle Bob sent a real sweet card. Nearly broke my heart," I lied. "Said to tell Daddy to blow off some M-80's in the backyard in memory of Jebo."

After we hung up, I straightened the stack of *Ladies' Home Journals* and *National Geographics* on the coffee table and then eased down onto the sectional sofa to kill time. The crumpled note in my pocket poked at my leg. I took it out and ironed it flat with my hand. The black words wore a hole in my brain. In between episodes of *Mayberry R.F.D.* on TV, I must have reread that stupid note twenty times. "RECORD POEMS ONTO CASSETTE."

After pouring another cup of coffee, I studied my distorted reflection in the muddy pond and flared my nostrils. Cupping the mug, I returned to Jebo's room. The tape recorder waved from the top of her dresser. "RECORD POEMS." . . . *That's ridiculous*, I thought.

Something rumbled in the driveway. Aunt Edna was dragging two maple dining room chairs from the storage shed across the asphalt to her car. Daddy would've given the chairs to her if she'd just asked. Edna secured the open trunk with a polka-dotted necktie. I heard the Pacer pull away from the curb while I started to read another poem.

Nickie Pickle's Momma

The first time I laid eyes on
Nickie Pickle's momma
she was strutting to the snack bar,

—a two-piece
leopard-print bathing suit.

Ten push-ups
on the concrete beside the pool
draw boys' eyes like flies
before she orders curly fries and a co-cola.
Melon bosoms swim
beneath her leopard skin.
Red sling-backs
dig dark marks
in the close-cut grass.

The only other time I saw Ms. Pickle
in that tight-fitting getup
was the day Daddy caught her
sunbathing on the haunches
of my quarter horse
outside the cover of cottonwood trees.

Slathering Coppertone on
casual-like:
"How's your family?"
or "Do you think we'll get a storm?"
Like my daddy wouldn't fall for her
high atop the horse.
Momma home in ugly pink curlers
slicing a rump roast,

smoking herself into a bass.
—Truth be told
she should've sung alto.

It was Nickie Pickle's momma
that brought on every bit
of that summer's drama.

Momma acted like she didn't care
that Daddy fell on Ms. Pickle way up there.
Until she split-cracked her skull
on a home-canned jar of cucumbers.

If the heart won't break,
the mind'll shatter in a million pieces.

Still spit-picks the glass shards
from her graying gums.

I hate the name Nickie Pickle
about as bad as I hate her momma.

Her face was unforgettable—big and horsey. Those spider-leg false eye-lashes, and a pancake-bronze foundation line that abruptly stopped at the jaw against her lily-white neck. Levelda was her real name. She claimed that she retired as a torch-song singer because of her smoker's cough. Saturday mornings she'd drop by the furniture store—a D cup beneath her leopard-print top—and hack into a

Kleenex. Never bought a thing. Just sat up on a white-canopied bed in the back corner of the store and flirted.

Jebo's poems confirmed my suspicions around the breakup of Uncle Billy's marriage. Why hadn't Momma told me the truth?

Even though I couldn't help but laugh, "Nickie Pickle's Momma" tasted lonesome and bitter in my mouth.

August 5, 1977—It's hot as hades. The wall unit blew up. Too hot to finish this poem. We've got to get somebody out here to fix it. May Dean's been fairly stable here lately. Her medicine must be working. Penny Sue's what worries me. Yesterday she froze up when that woman at church asked her what was wrong with her aunt, Edna. I should have jumped in and rescued her, but I wanted to see what she said. Penny Sue just studied the floor, didn't say a word. Tell her she's special, I thought. Tell 'em anything. May Dean's made such a big deal out of "don't tell our family business." Penny soaked it up like a sponge. May Dean's holding us all hostage trying to keep it a secret. Hell, I'd never say it to her face, but that woman's got "crazy ass" written all over her. I bought Penny Sue one of those 8-track tape players.

I closed the book and heard Jebo's voice again, speaking the words of the poem. "If the heart won't break, the mind'll shatter in a million pieces."

Eleven

All I did the next three days was traipse around the house reading Jebo's diaries. They gripped me by the back of the neck and stood me up in front of memories that I'd conveniently chosen to forget.

March 1, 1983—We got an inch of snow. Penny Sue eloped with Darrell over in Arkansas. He's been singing some on the weekends over at the VFW in Barlett. I don't think it pays a dime. I didn't recognize her when they stopped by the house. She kept fiddling with the wedding ring on her finger.

July 20, 1983—Month-long drought. Evidently the honeymoon's over. Darrell's down in the dumps. He drove all the way over to Nashville to hear some big-shot record executive set him straight about his singing. Man said he was a decent tenor but should stick to church choir. Told him not to bother coming back because he didn't have the "look" they wanted. Penny said it hit him real hard and he's taking it out on her. She's bending over backwards to try and make him happy. Whatever Darrell wants Darrell gets as far as she's concerned. Penny Sue covered for him when he didn't come to the 4th of July party. Says he's just restless these days. Darrell wants her at home cooking and cleaning for him. Porter's thinking about selling the furniture store. I'm going to play canasta with Luna tonight. I hope Penny Sue's all right. I asked her to sit down and play guitar with me the other night and she said she didn't play anymore. I worked on my poems.

December 24, 1988—Temperatures got below freezing last night. Christmas Eve. I gave everybody socks. The striped kind that work like gloves—a place to put every toe. Of course, Edna brought her accordion over as usual. Made my famous rum cake. I saw Stella Prine take three pieces home under her car coat. That's gluttonous if you ask me. Darrell acted up as usual. Porter made him leave the house. Penny confided in me. He's still drinking like a fish and won't let her go out by herself. I told her there's things much worse than divorce. This cough is nagging me.

May 25, 1989—Breezy and mild. Bigmouth Stella Prine called this morning. Penny Sue suspected something was going on with Darrell but she didn't know what. Now she knows. That marriage has beaten her down. Good riddance. Stella wouldn't get off the phone without asking if I'd seen a doctor about my cough. I don't need anybody telling me what to do.

I was wearing a path in the carpet going back and forth to Jebo's room to read. Her words were like water from a well. Sometimes I'd carry the diaries around the house out in front of me like a divining rod. To tell the truth (isn't that an odd notion?), something deep inside me knew that I couldn't get on with my life until I'd read all those diaries.

Ghosted

His manufactured housing's haunted
by a spouse who's wanting something
she can't get up the gumption to ask for.

Pacing plastic runners
in a hooded, white, terry-cloth bathrobe
rattling her ball and chain.
Hoping he'll speak her name.
It's Lorraine.

You kind of lose yourself
when your name ain't called
and your face ain't seen,
your beauty gets buried,
know what I mean?

Truth be told, he hasn't summoned her since
he "Damn you, Lorraine"'d her

at the Chili Cook-off fire hall fund-raiser
(loaded his bowl
full of Tabasco).

He'd made a ghost of her
staring straight through her
at the TV, nursing Buds,
acting in public like he didn't know
who on earth she was.

Fried up the heart of her hand
in a cast-iron skillet
wondering if maybe
she could still feel it.
Poor Lorraine.

You kinda lose something
when your name ain't called
and your face ain't seen,
your beauty gets buried,
know what I mean?

Just a docile haint
in a hand-hewn jail—
that match made in heaven's
become a living hell
for this see-through lady

folded up on a hideaway bed.
The roving face of the oscillating fan,
one lazy eye, her mechanical friend,
tracks every move.

One night, she stands before that fan—
its face a cage between her hands,
spits each letter
clickity clackity click
into the electric breeze.

La a a a rai ai ai n n
        La a a rai rai nnn.

You finally lose something
when your name ain't called
and your face ain't seen,
your beauty's been buried,
know what I mean?

Call my name,   call my name,   it's Lorraine.

Jebo visited Darrell and me in Memphis. Brought her brand-new Tammy Wynette record. Wearing red boots with that denim skirt and top. Darrell asked her to take off the cowboy hat during supper. She wouldn't—said it made her feel safe. We slept together on the pullout. She forgot her toothbrush and borrowed mine. Jebo wrote in her little spiral book while we ate spaghetti. Darrell got mad. Not

about the writing; I think it was because she kept on picking up the
needle on the stereo and playing "D-I-V-O-R-C-E."

The words of the poem smacked up against the wall. I laid
the diary down on the bed. I had wanted something from
Darrell, something that he didn't have to give. Looking back,
I see that all that talk about a singing career was just a pau-
per's prayer. Darrell's dream made him a somebody; without
it, he was a nobody in his mind. When he let it go, he closed
his heart. Wouldn't even look me in the eye anymore after he
came back from Nashville. I nearly lost my mind. The next
thing you know I heard myself screaming at the diaries as if
the books were Jebo herself.

"I'm right here! I am caught inside every one of these,
Jebo. Did you know me better than I know myself? What in
the world am I supposed to do with all this?"

I needed air, some wide-open space big enough to hold all
the feelings that poem had let loose in my body.

⁓

The fire tower stood skeletal and stark there on the grassy rise
at the end of Buffalo Road. Reminded me of some addled,
gray soldier, bones without skin, put out to pasture, empty
beer cans flung around his feet.

My car rocked on its shocks turning into the gravel parking
lot. Cold wind slapped me awake, clearer than I'd been in
days. I covered my head with the yellow hood of my sweatshirt. Beneath my feet, dead leaves crunched, crackled. Tennis

shoes would have worked better than these pink flip-flops; my toes were going numb.

I flashed to a time years ago on a family picnic—Momma's expressionless face as she passed me a Dixie cup of sulfur-water Kool-Aid. That was back before they got us hooked up to city water. That image bled into "Penny Sue Pritchett loves Darrell Sykes," written in black Magic Marker on the fire tower.

I lifted my eyes to follow the lines of the fire tower's scaffolding, crisscrossed two-by-fours angled inward from a wide base. Three sets of ladders led the way to the top perch. Used to, I could nearly run up the rungs. Not today.

With a book bag full of Jebo's diaries slung over my shoulder, I began to climb the gray soldier's skeletal system. The weight of the books whopped my knees every time I lifted my leg up the rotting rungs. An old song Jebo taught me came on in my head.

Toe bone's connected to the foot bone . . . foot bone's connected to the anklebone . . . anklebone's connected . . .

I need to get out of the house more, I thought.

The gaps of the wooden planks on the first landing showed the ground below. I didn't stop but made an angled about-face to head up the second set of steps.

Shinbone's connected to the knee bone . . . knee bone's connected to the thighbone . . . thigh bone's connected to the hip bone . . .

A crow's cry shot the distance between us, causing me to slip and scrape my knee on one of the ladder rungs.

"Shut up, bird."

The scrape hurt like the dickens, but it didn't bleed. Hand over hand, foot upon foot I climbed. Wasps had a nest under the second landing. I'm allergic so I quickly moved forward.

Backbone's connected to the shoulder bone . . . shoulder bone's connected to the neck bone . . . neck bone's connected to the head bone . . .

The third landing was wider, enough for three or four people to sit, like a widow's walk. The railing, torn away on one side, was rotted. I laid the book bag on the graying boards and turned to look out over the tree line. I'd always been too scared to come to the top like this—never had seen the view. It was like a poem: leaves clung to trees in scarlet, orange, and yellow; a cotton field plucked clean except for scattered white speckles. Overhead, the serrated edge of a hawk's wing circled toward the sun. I nearly lost my balance when the wind gusted, so I sat down to steady myself.

I searched the scaffolding for the inscription: "Penny Sue Pritchett loves Darrell Sykes." There it was; the names had faded to dusty smudges, dirt daubers' nests covered the spot.

I pulled diary #2 from the green bag. Jebo's best friend, Luna, taught me a trick she did with the Bible. Said it always worked. She'd let the Scriptures fall open and randomly point to a verse. Luna assumed that whatever she found on the page was meant for her to hear that day. I decided to do the same thing with the diary. I let it fall open, closed my eyes, and pointed to this poem:

Dixie's Landline

Born with a voice husky and low
could'a been a DJ
on AM radio
if her ole man
let her work outside
the home.

Aunt Dixie's dream
never came to pass,
tonight she'll close those eyes
and raise that glass,
"Breaker breaker 1-9
I got your mighty fine wine
a c'mon."

Trucker talk's her hot cup of tea,
on a sagging card table
sets her landline CB radio
with a push-bar silver microphone.

Privacy's a commodity
undercut in this house by poverty
so Dixie carries on in front of us kids.
"Breaker breaker 1-9
Fryin' you some bacon
Scramblin' eggs

Serving up some of Dixie dregs
a c'mon."

Dixie hollers out,
"Look away from me, kids."
Telling bold-faced lies
when the honest truth is:
she's wooing truckers
hauling produce
and Batesville caskets
barreling through the Ozarks.

She forbids our eyes
so our ears misconstrue.
If you'd a stood there with us
you'd a heard it too,
"Brake her, break her . . . one time."

"Raven-haired; I'm a raving beauty,"
she purrs to anybody in the vicinity.
"Hauling postholes, honey.
10-4, Backdoor,
put the pedal to the metal,
and let 'er roar."

Sweet nothings
negotiate Arkansas airwaves,
behind stacked-up cereal boxes

she sips Ripple and plays
old LPs to road scholars
turning the pages of night.

For one ole boy
on a cross-country excursion
she sings without the record,
an a cappella version
crooning, "Moon river . . . wider than a mile."
(Crossing her heart in the style of the Catholics
though we know she ain't nothin'
but a cradle Church of Christ.)

    "Breaker, breaker 1-9
    nothing on but the radio."

Love the art, not the artist,
they always say.
So we close our eyes,
enjoy the music,
and look away
look away
look away from Dixie's landline.

"Breaker, breaker
1-9.
Brake her, break her one time?"

I'd forgotten all about her until now. Momma's younger sister Dixie used to send me a birthday card every year with five dollars inside. We visited her house one summer. Curtains drawn made it dark even in the daytime. She hunkered over what looked like a makeshift radio station; a turntable, a microphone. Her husband came home unexpectedly. Momma hurried me out to the car. That next year, cards stopped coming. Momma said she died. We never went to a funeral. I didn't know whether to believe Momma or not.

And then there was that underlining again, Jebo signaling another entry for me to read.

April 1970—The daffodils are up. Mid-70s today. Penny Sue won't wear her glasses to Mitchell - Neilson Elementary. She'd rather sit there and squint at the chalkboard. Mrs. Maybry, her second-grade teacher, called for a conference. Porter and May Dean went over without me. I wanted to go too, but it didn't seem right. You'd a thought Penny Sue committed a crime by the sound of Mrs. Maybry's voice on the phone. Porter let me read the progress report. In a nutshell all it said was "Penny Sue chews the ends of her pencils." "Crunches ice constantly." "She's shy with the other kids." But her grades looked real good. Two As, two Bs, and a C. Her teacher's worried about Penny Sue crying when she asked the question, "How's your family doing?"

September 1973—Tornado warnings. I pulled the twin mattress into the bathtub downstairs in case we have to take shelter tonight. One's already touched down over in Shelby County. Penny Sue's acting funny. She caught me having a good cry yesterday. I should have said something but I was just too big of a mess. I mean boo-hooing. Felt like my heart broke apart inside my chest. Every time I think about Howard, I come undone. Still feel like I did the right thing, but Lord knows I miss him something awful. Sometimes I wonder what would have happened if I'd a just left Porter and Penny Sue and run off with him like he wanted. I could never leave Penny Sue with her—May Dean's still too fragile. I'm not even sure Howard's divorce was final. I think that was my last shot at love. There never was a lotta love in my marriage to the children's father.

Back on solid ground, riding in the car to Momma and Daddy's house, I banged on the dashboard where my radio used to be. What was I supposed to do with all this, I wondered. The stupid note in my pocket made it crystal clear what I was supposed to do—RECORD POEMS. As strange as it seemed to me after reading and entering the world of Jebo's poems, I seriously considered the request. Something otherworldly, beyond the walls, seemed to be driving me to follow the directions to the letter.

Twelve

In the dream I am hovering above a hospital room—stark white walls, icky fluorescent lighting, and one of those iron single beds from institutions in the '60s—watching a younger version of me down below. The younger me is wearing all white—her arms are pinned and crossed upon her chest; the long white coat sleeves tied around behind her back. I realize that she, me, is in a straitjacket and has consented to be restrained. Blue masking tape covers her mouth.

The younger me fights her way out of bed, waddles to the window, knocks over the IV stand, and purple liquid oozes onto the floor. Sitting on the windowsill is a small black tape recorder. A gravelly male voice says, "I dare you, Penny Sue." I'm still hovering, watching the younger me down below.

At this point the dream feels dangerous. The younger me struggles to turn off the recorder but realizes her hands are pinned to her sides. "Find someone to help you turn it over," says the male voice. On the bottom of the recorder is a large red circle. All the younger me needs to do is press the red circle and speak into the microphone and the ominous voice will be satisfied. The younger me can't press the button while her hands are tied and her mouth is taped over.

Then, the older me that has been hovering up in the corner glides down through the air like a ghost and lands on the floor beside the younger me and says, "I'm here to help you." The grown-up me moves close to the microphone and reaches out to press the red button—no idea what to say. All the older me can think of is "Testing" and says it a second time with a British accent. "Testing, testing" The dream feels scary until I speak, and then it shifts. The third time I say "Testing," I get tickled and laugh. That is when I must have woken myself up, giggling.

When I awoke from the dream I rolled over onto my back, expecting to see the hospital room. Instead, there's a white wicker chair beside the bed and Grand Ole Opry stars overhead. I had been sleeping on my stomach with both arms trapped beneath me and they'd fallen asleep. I clumsily clapped them together to get the blood flowing again. As they started to buzz I recounted my dream. The message seemed obvious. What was I waiting for? After I got up and brushed my teeth for the first time in a couple of days, I took Jebo's tape recorder off the dresser and placed it on the bed. Angling the little microphone toward me, I drew a deep breath and pressed the Record button. My voice was steadier than usual.

Aunt Shine's Face-Lift

Ever since she was a child
she took real pains with her looks.
Shine saved the surgeon's scalpel and sutures,

they lie prostrate in her chewing gum drawer—
reverent accoutrements of the arts
of tying down the hands of time.

Aunt Shine's face-lift, still swollen,
cost an arm and a leg.
She crammed it on her credit card.
Cleans office buildings at night
to pay the doctor bill:
smoothing creases
drawing blinds
vacuuming fuzz off the floor.
Somehow she's stitching
the payments together.

I admit, she looked decent
at Big Momma's funeral;
an injected stillness
froze the muscles
of her usually furrowed brow.

And now, back in the kitchen
cousins gnaw neck bones and shelly beans.
I caught 'em fiddlin'
with the grandfather clock,
trying to trick us into eating early
after the burial.
They changed time in secret,

like those skin surgeons haggled over
Big Momma's grown-child's face.

Big Momma lifted Shine's face
as a child,
whispered, "You are wild, girl,
you are perfect,
and you are mine."
I guess it's true that we cain't "reteach
a thing its loveliness?"
Say what you will . . .
the distance has been distorted,
the distance
between our family's living
and our family's dead.

It's like I held the memory in the dead center of my chest cavity. The sting of Momma's hand across my cheek. I'm eleven or twelve years old. We are putting up the groceries in that long cabinet next to the broom closet. Butter beans were boiling over and making a hissing sound. All I did was ask Momma why Reverend Cutie Wallace's wife looked like she'd pinned her face back. I might have said that it looked like Saran wrap pulled tight across a bowl of leftovers. I figured Momma got mad because Reverend Wallace had just bought a hundred church pews from Daddy. It was all so confusing.

A slant light across the window grid cast a long cross-shaped shadow on the floor in Jebo's room. My eighth-grade

Sunday school teacher had once used the word *deworlded*; floored me for some reason. No idea what it meant until that very moment. I was walking in no-man's-land.

Too bad we can't reteach a girl her loveliness.

"Amen," I said and nodded through murky tears.

For a moment I wondered if I'd left the bedside radio playing in Jebo's room, but it was just the sound track coming on in my head again. This time without meaning to, I spun the George Jones record "He Stopped Loving Her Today." I wished I had a button in my brain to turn it off, but I didn't. So, with the song blaring in the background, I picked up the tape recorder and placed it back on top of Jebo's dresser.

Jebo's presence was growing stronger with each poem. I felt like I was being yanked off to someplace I wasn't sure that I was ready to go. I feared there might be no turning back.

By the time I walked back downstairs darkness swallowed the house. When I flipped the light switch, fluorescents blinded me; the blinds on the windows wide open so I pulled them shut. Hoping nobody was peeping in because they'd get an ugly eyeful for sure. My dirty blond hair was going ever-which-a-way. For the past few days the idea of a bath had only struck me from a distance.

The images these poems conjured, ached. It was as if the actual pictures in my head hurt. I wasn't sure that I could hold another word, but I felt like my life depended upon these journal entries and poems. I picked up diary #3 and cradled it to my heart. Invisible hands around my throat made it hard to swallow. For years I'd numbed any physical symptoms of sadness, drowning my grief beneath the liquid fire I drove down the back of my throat. It wasn't that I refused to speak the truth about my troubles, I wasn't even sure what they were. All of the secrets Momma kept from me caused me to lose hold of the thread running through my family's stories. Somewhere along the line I disconnected, unplugged the telephone, so to speak.

Shortly after I married Darrell my life had become a simple set of steps: wake up, drink coffee, wipe counters, fold clothes, vacuum floors, drive to Kmart, maybe buy Windex and Comet, come home, and sleep. Oh boy, had I ever slept.

Believe it or not, when Darrell and I first married and moved to Memphis I dreamed of owning my own beauty shop. Right now all I wanted was a regular paycheck. Boyd had cut back my hours. I was only working two days a week. The last time I hit a good lick was before Darrell and I split up. At the time I picked up a second job at the local country radio station, WGNS. The station manager hired me over the phone, said my voice would "sell," whatever that meant. All I did was read copy on drugstore and local bank commercials, but to tell the truth I liked hearing the sound of my voice on the radio. Lasted there six months to the day. Darrell razzed me every single time I started out the door for work.

"You think you're gonna be a famous radio personality?" The rant could go on and on.

"You think you're such a damn big shot, Penny Sue. You're nothing but an embarrassment," his huge arm above the door-frame hemming me in until he was through.

Darrell didn't make me quit my job; he just stayed on me, wore me down, until I did. My migraines got real bad after that.

Thirteen

Knock knock knock, came a loud pounding on the front door.

"Okay, hold on, I'm coming," I called.

The pounding only got louder.

"All right, I said. I'm coming."

There on the covered porch stood the mayor's wife, Luna Shackleford, like an elderly trick-or-treater. I flipped the light switch and opened the door. She was in midswing. Using the dog's water bowl as a knocker.

"What in the world is it, Ms. Luna?"

"I'll tell you 'what in the world,'" she said, brushing past my shoulder with insistent short steps, both hands full. "I've been standing out here banging on your door. You scared me. Thought you were locked up in here hollering for help."

"I'm sorry, Ms. Luna. I didn't hear you." I took the dog bowl from her hand and placed it on the kitchen floor.

"Look at you, Penny Sue. You've been holed up in here too long. Looks like the cat's been sucking on your hair. Your momma's mail was hanging out of the box." Jebo always said that Luna Shackleford was as good as gold and that she'd give you the purse off her arm if you really needed it.

Tucked under Luna's arm was a fat bundle of mail and in her hands, a Karo pecan pie. Luna Shackleford and Jebo played canasta together for years. Jebo and Luna would play cards for an entire weekend.

Luna was a spitfire, the type who at eighty-two still push-mowed her yard wearing little white Keds tennis shoes. She wore her honey-colored wig pulled down over her eyebrows. It might have been a little big. She styled it every Saturday at the Clip Joint on Highway 55. I knew all this because Jebo told me. Ms. Luna pressed the warm pie tin into my upturned hands and slid the mail bundle onto the kitchen table.

"You sure you're okay here all alone, child?" she asked after a noisy exhale, one eyebrow driven up under the front lip of her wig.

"Yes, ma'am," I answered. "Ms. Luna, listen to this, from Jebo's diary; you're in here:

September 1966—Indian summer. My garden didn't do flitter this year. Dry all summer. Spent the last few Saturday nights at the Moose Lodge WITH LUNA. [I emphasized her name with wide eyes, all dramatic.] *Won the bingo pot. She wanted to give her part away to the custodian up at her church. I'm hoping to sing on the Lodge stage one night. Worried about May Dean. Porter's traveling. She can't sleep at night. She ran over some dog in front of the hardware store. Caused a ruckus but nobody hurt except the dog! Arthur Penwell stopped me in the grocery store and said that May Dean's eyes were wild after the wreck. Then got a call from Stella last week wanting to know why May Dean was outside with no shirt on. I've gotta talk to Porter when he gets back.*

"Do you remember that, Ms. Luna? Do you remember playing bingo with Jebo at the Moose Lodge? Do you remember my momma running over that dog?"

I glanced up to find Luna frozen on the spot, a funny look in her eyes. Quickly she went back to her fluttering around the kitchen.

"I reckon," she said. "That was long ago, child. Don't feed your dog on the front porch, hear? It's trashy."

"Yes, ma'am," I said. The smell of the pie she'd brought reminded me I'd neglected to eat much and my blood sugar must be wavering. "And thank you for the pie."

"Well, I hope y'all enjoy it. Sure do miss your Jebo." She started to say something else but hesitated, then covered her mouth with her hand and shook her head back and forth disappointedly and walked away from the door.

"Thank-you, Ms. Luna," I called behind her. "I'll be sure and tell Momma you brought the pie."

Ms. Luna adjusted her wig like she'd tipped her hat, spun on her heel, and dissolved into the darkness.

I looked down at the jumble of envelopes. Buried in the middle of the stack of mail was another prison-orange one, type-addressed to me.

"Come back anytime, Ms. Luna" missed her completely as she slammed the door of her champagne Mercury Marquis.

For a few seconds the envelope burned into my hand. One of Ms. Luna's car lights was out, so a single bright eye wandered and shrank as she snaked back down the drive. As soon as the light disappeared I tore off the end. My eyes drank in the large printed words, cut out and pasted on the white card stock.

HAVE YOU tAPED thE POEMS?
IF SO, PUT tOGEThER YOUR
   COStUME
sOMEthING OLD sOMEthING NEW
sOMEthING BORROWED,
sOMEthING ! ! !

The blonde hairs on my arms stood straight up. What kind of lunatic would ransom my Jebo's diaries? And was I insane enough to obey?

Heat lightning flashed outside, but the skies held their water. I couldn't sleep. I thought about taking some of Momma's nerve pills but decided against it. The bedcovers irritated my skin, I couldn't get comfortable. Frantically, I got up out of bed and started pacing the floor.

"You gonna wear a hole in my good carpet, girl." I could hear Momma complain as I went back and forth.

I tore down the stairs, trying to get away. Air in the house was thick. Momma and Daddy were safety nuts; they'd nailed the den windows shut.

The hammer was in the garage inside Daddy's red-metal sectioned toolbox. I hauled the heavy box back into the den just in case I needed another tool, pried the nails from the frames, and threw open the windows. Strong gusts of wind churned dry leaves outside. A large limb snapped and shook the ground like a throbbing bass note. High winds usually scared me, but tonight their building intensity matched my own state of mind. Windows wide open, white sheers whipping around the room, wild, like dancing ghosts. The rain would be here in a minute. A nearby crack of thunder sent a shot of adrenaline straight through me.

I tangled in the blowing sheers, twisting in them until they pulled off the rod. I spun around and around, hollering like those Appalachian conjure women Jebo'd told me about. My unhealed big toe caught on the coffee table where Daddy still had President Reagan's picture slid up under the glass. Fire shot up through my calf. My foot on fire, I hopped to the window, threw my head back and howled my maiden name at the top of my lungs into the wild evening breeze.

"Penny Sue Pritchett. Penny Sue Pritchett! What the hell happened to you?! Where did you go?"

In my head I heard music, but this time it was Jebo on her Gibson guitar accompanying the frenzied scene. The truth she was revealing to me in her diaries wasn't sweet. It was more bitter like blood. But for the first time in years I was breaking open. Some of my vague memories were making sense. Up until now I'd deferred to Momma's version of the truth.

Fourteen

Morning brought relief. The State Farm Insurance calendar in Jebo's bedroom had October 31 circled in orange Magic Marker. Halloween was days away. The diary beckoned. I turned to the next entry she'd underlined.

October 15, 1980 — It hung in the low 70s all day. Penny graduates from high school this year. She got the lead in HMS Pinafore. *We're sick to death of the song "I'm Called Little Buttercup," must have heard it a thousand times out there in the backyard. May Dean's nerves are acting up. She may not be able to go to the show. I'm proud as a peacock of Penny Sue. She took my suggestion and tried out on Ronnie Milsap's "It Was Almost Like a Song." Hope she goes to college. She's real good on the stage. Porter says he'll pay for it. I think she's got her mind set on beauty school.*

Remembering that year, the year I sang onstage, was almost funny to me. How had I ever been that person? How had I lost touch with that? I laughed out loud at the thought.

Still riding the wild wave of last night's storm, I found myself standing barefoot in front of Jebo's closet.

Tucked into a cubbyhole on the right side of the closet was a large plastic ziplock bag containing several Sears professional portraits Jebo had had taken of herself. Every three or four years she wanted to see if the photographer could capture "her essence," was the way she put it. She loved a swimsuit shot.

"Will wonders never cease?" I mimicked Jebo's favorite line.

I pulled out a picture of her in front of a faux waterwheel backdrop. Jebo stood with her hand on her hip wearing a burnt orange shirtwaist dress that zipped up the side. If you looked closely, you could see little owls in the material print. She wore an earnest look that conflicted with the ridiculousness of her surroundings. Her lips were drawn back into a straight line. Her piercing blue eyes blazed. The most striking part was her hair.

I remembered the story she told about how she'd diluted some Clorox in a paint can. She'd tested the mixture on the dog several times before painting a white streak, zigzag, down the front of her bangs. I remember it because she asked me to bring home a strip of cotton balls from the barber college that weekend to keep the bleach out of her eyes. In her letter to me, she said it was the day she decided her destiny. She called the hairstyle the White Lightning.

I held the picture up toward the window. I'd *borrow* this *old* dress and it would be *new* to me. I'd found my costume.

⌒

Jebo was a packrat, never threw anything away. After a bit of searching, I found the orange-print dress deep in the left side of the closet. I liked the thought of me in this dress. All I needed was a pair of quarter-inch bone pumps to complete my getup. A long rectangular mirror hung on the back of the closet door. I measured the dress length by holding the hanger chin-high and studying my reflection. Jebo's poem from her first diary came back to me.

Sorrow Knows This Dress

Sorrow knows this dress,
cotton-made, time-torn.
It's not the color or the cut that cries out
but the slack-shouldered emptiness, a scarecrow
exposed to a parched dusty yard.
Reveals more than a housedress should.
Around the hemline, shame shows.
Embarrassed, a shy collarbone
protrudes. Pale daisy-print cloth,
forgetful now of summer days
blowing on the line between the sweet gums.
Bosoms nag at the waistline—
hungry old mares.
Belly slack from childbearing

and buttered bread.
The knees poke through,
cotton worn so thin it shines.
I wrestle this place—
this cotton-field-of-a-dress.

*The clinic lady drove me home from school at lunchtime because I
had a stomachache. Jebo must have thought she was all alone in the
house. Daddy'd just carpeted the stairs so she didn't hear me when
I came up them, "Anybody here? I'm home."*

   *The door to her room was slightly ajar. Jack Greene was croon-
ing "There Goes My Everything" on her radio. Through the crack in
the door I saw her kneeling in front of the small closet. Two cinna-
mon candles flickered on the bedside table. From the back it looked
like she had her face buried in the bottom half of a silky white dress
I'd never seen her wear before. Her shoulders heaved up and down.
She was braying somebody's name. I think it was Howard. I didn't
know anybody named Howard. I went back downstairs and waited
for her on the couch. I'd never seen her cry like that before.*

The poem really rattled my cage. I had been wrestling the
place that I came from for years.

~

I went over and over the poems. Learned several of them
by heart. I liked to imagine hearing Jebo's voice reading my
favorite lines.

"A young girl can't fathom what a hard woman knows" . . . "If the heart won't break, the mind'll shatter in a million pieces" . . .

The words must have tripped a switch in my brain, because the sound track cranked up right as I said them. I recognized the song as Lynn Anderson's "Rose Garden."

"I beg your pardon, I never promised you a rose garden." Jebo had written the line in the margin of the first diary. I sang along with Lynn, "Along with the sunshine, there's gotta be a little rain sometime."

The music was like a limb hanging over the side of a rushing river, and I latched on. With the truth of the fiction I was reading and the music my own body seemed to provide, even my breathing had slowed and I was finding a calmness, a peace I hadn't known I was missing.

It was like I had stumbled onto the varied notes and tempo of Jebo's strong musical soul in a new way. The more poems I read, the more she seemed like several people all rolled into one. I liked how she'd written down actual events in her life and shaped them into something more. It was like she saw clean through what was happening in her life and captured the bigger picture. Every time I read one, I discovered more about her. Or more about myself.

⌐

The doorbell rang. A dark-headed fella in a UPS uniform cupped his hand over one eye to cut the glare off the glass and peered into the narrow pane beside the front door. There were gaps between his teeth. When he smiled his tongue looked like a prisoner behind white bars. He saw me see him, and snapped back to attention. As I was opening the door, he called me by my maiden name.

"Miss Penny Sue Pritchett?"

I nodded. "Yes."

"Need your John Hancock on this line," he said, handing me a clipboard and pen, nervously running large hands through oily black hair. His aftershave was so pungent I breathed out of my mouth. I signed and traded him the clipboard for the certified letter. His parting smile seemed to indicate we'd made some sort of pact, the nature of which eluded me.

The envelope wasn't prison orange like the last two. This time the ransom writer chose a powder baby-blue, same upside-down Eddie Eagan stamp every time. Who knows, maybe the color change signaled that the charades were coming to a close. The paper nicked my finger as I worked it under the adhesive on the envelope. While I put my mouth to my finger to suck the little drop of blood, the sound track boomed from out of nowhere. The shaky start to "Wake Up, Little Susie" on my head-radio made me smile.

Inside the envelope I found the same large print. The note read:

sHOWTiME.
3rd AND FINAL ReqUEST

bRIng RECORDED POEMS tO
PLAY AT family reunion
BE In FUIL COSTUME
PLAY POEMS OVER sOUND
SYSTEM
AND the sECrets OF thE 4Th
dIaRY
MAY BE YOUrs

The telephone rang as I read the last line. I picked up halfway through the second ring.

"Hello."

"Penny Sue?"

"Darrell?"

"Yeah. Penny, I don't know how to tell you this. I've been trying to get up the nerve to call for days, and I didn't—"

"Did you send these notes?" I interrupted him.

"What?"

"Darrell, why would you want to scare me like this?"

"I don't know what you're talking about. I heard that your Jebo died, and I wanted to tell you how sorry I am."

"Huh?"

"I stopped by the furniture store and your uncle Billy told me."

"Why didn't you send a card or something?"

"I thought about it but haven't gotten around to it yet."

"So are you the one sending these stupid notes?"

"What? Penny, I said I wanted to say I'm sorry. Maybe we can talk?"

"What's that noise?"

A young child's tiny voice said "hello" on the other end of the line.

"Get off the phone, kids!" Darrell shouted, angry that he'd been caught.

"Why are you calling me when you're still living over there?" I slammed the receiver down so hard the mouthpiece popped off. Nothing had changed. The room spun. It was like I'd left the blacktop at high speed and I was in some freshly plowed field, wheels spinning. I guess all along I'd hoped these notes were from Darrell and that he was working his way back. I felt foolish for following the line of the notes. I was still stuck. Nothing had changed. "Get ahold of yourself, Penny Sue."

I reached for the grounding rod of the diary.

Rich Man Poor Man Timber Man Drunk

How is it, a dark, dashing daddy—
a drunk—who pours timber paychecks down
a silver flask strapped to his hobbled leg—
can walk out of the woods weekly
sloshed, a hero, belt-buckling the backsides
of the eight he sired but never daddied,
take a passing slap at their mother
as she returns ragged from the cotton field,

that night defile a daughter silently
blaming it all on devil moonshine;
then thirty years down the road
rock on that same girl's porch
dying of lung cancer
calling himself
to her children
—in front of her own fried chicken
a grand-daddy of 'em all?
Tell me that.

The blades of the overhead fan rhythmically sliced the air. During Jebo's lifetime, I'd heard his name, Orville Shigley, cross her lips once. Shingley was Jebo's maiden name. I remember the way the turnip greens smelled on the stove and the bobby pin falling out of her hair in the back. Her eyes were wild.

She said, "Daddy cut timber for a living, ran a sawmill outside Jonesboro, at the foot of the Ozarks. His paycheck never made it past the bootleg liquor store. My sisters and I hired out as cleaning ladies by the time we were thirteen years old."

Momma heard Jebo talking and came in to stop her from telling me any more. Jebo kept right on talking.

"I lied to a man so he'd marry me. Told him I was twenty-one and I wasn't even sixteen yet. He didn't know the truth until I got pregnant and we got married."

Momma told me to go back in my room.

Jebo wouldn't talk about it after that.

I dragged myself down the hall to the bathroom. Imagining Jebo's face as a young girl as the old-time house band in my head began to play "Devil in the Woodpile." I turned on the shower. The knob squeeked. The music was different this time—menacing, distorted and loud. It soon became deafening. I covered my ears but only trapped the tune inside my head.

I tried to escape by climbing into the black-tiled stall and closing the filmy glass door behind me, but I couldn't stop the song. Jebo's young face faded into the thickening steam. The full force of the realization washed over me as the hot water burned my back. I pinned my body flat against the tile to avoid the scalding water; then with the tip of my finger I slowly inscribed the song title into the condensation on the black tile wall. My finger lingered there pointing at the culprit. It was a revealed secret my grandmother and I had never divulged to each other face-to-face—Devil in the Woodpile.

Frozen tears shattered like glass as they fell. Shards cut my face and chest, nicked my legs and then snagged going down the drain. The "devil in my woodpile" was a boy cousin, killed young in a head-on collision. He had forced me into the storage room out back of the garage when I was eleven, wedged a pine board against the door. A purple hula hoop hung on a nail behind his head; the beads made a rain sound as I frantically swatted for something to hold on to. I never told a soul. I'd buried that memory like a snake in the backyard. So deep in the dirt, it only hissed at night in hideous dreams.

Had Jebo somehow suspected all along?

Sitting, curled up on the shower floor, I let the water run until it turned cold. I remember the mildew between the tiles, and thinking, *It'll never come clean, none of it.* I was terrified of losing control. Jebo's words, the long reach of her spirit, wrapped around me and I cried harder. She was more alive to me now than ever.

Looking back, it was there in the shower, after my body stopped shaking, that the music in my head shut off for good. Never heard it again, it stopped as abruptly as it started.

❧

Leaning my head down to twist the soft white towel around my hair, the room spun. When I was little Jebo taught me to follow my breath down into my belly when I needed to regain control. More than once over the years that lesson had been a lifesaver. As I leaned back up I stared at my puffy eyes, bloodshot and swollen, in the mirror. My skin looked baby pink; it surprised me. It was fresh-looking—as if I'd somehow shed a skin.

It was like the poems had a mouth and they soon called to me.

When Are You Coming Home, Girl?

Momma lit out for college, 1953
warming a Greyhound bus seat,
and a sack of dreams.

She traces the driver's tattoo
on my arm every time
she tells the story.

Chess squares, in cheesecloth
soak her Samsonite suitcase,
a soiled note her momma wrote
said, "When you coming home, girl, soon?"

She tells how my daddy dazzled her
kicking quarters
into his shirt pocket
in the lunch line
the second week of school.

Next thing she knew
he'd bought a ring
—couldn't afford the thing.
She quit school to marry.

"Let's leave this hellhole,"
he hollered,
"dusty squalor, all of it."

His Impala down Highway 24
he swore he'd make a doctor,
a lawyer, a junk bond salesman,
or a hotel developer.

Grandma lit her heart afire,
set it in the windowsill—
mouthing prayers at
Momma's senior picture.

"When you coming home, girl,
when you coming home?"
Daddy gave her
a house to keep
kids to raise
a yard to mow
an old clunker car
to go places
she'd never seen before.

Before long Momma's northern star
dropped from her
housedress pockets
onto the linoleum.

On cold nights, here in this drafty kitchen
crickets pinch her nerves
Viceroys soothe her soul.
Momma still aches to answer
the call across the years,

"When you coming home girl,
When you coming home?"

*Jebo and I had stopped by Luna Shackleford's house to eat cupcakes
after my ball team won the church league city championship. I was
disappointed because Momma wouldn't get up off the couch to
come and see me play. When we got to Luna's she was back in the
bedroom, her ankle propped up on some pillows, making telephone
calls to the other elderly shut-ins at church. She'd turned her ankle
falling off the Shoney's sidewalk. Jebo went back in Luna's room to
see about her. I overheard their conversation.*

"How long has she been on the couch?"

*"Luna, May Dean's doing the best she can under the circum-
stances," Jebo said.*

*I never asked Jebo what she meant by "under the circumstances,"
but I never forgot the surprising tenderness in her voice.*

I walked down the hall and back into Jebo's room holding
#3, closing the distance between myself and the other two
diaries. Fanning my face with the front flap, I walked out on
the little porch that led off her room. The gentle breeze of
her words was like a cool hand on my fevered forehead, very
different from the touch of the tough-skinned, trash-talking
woman I knew growing up.

The fourth diary was gonna be mine. In my bones I knew
that I'd be there at the family reunion, wearing Jebo's dress and
playing the poems I'd recorded. Jebo's words had become my
lifeline, a lifeline I would follow hand over hand to the shore.

Fifteen

The strip mall housed four stores: a Fred's Discount, Buy-Low Fabrics, some little knickknack place, and Becker's Army Navy Surplus. I had seen in the paper where Fred's was having a sale, and so I went in to buy a change of clothes.

"Ma'am." I hailed a salesclerk then followed her down the aisle. "Ma'am, can you help me?"

When she spun around the name tag pinned to her red smock read "Regina," though I'd just overheard another clerk with a wet mop call her Tonya.

"How much you want to spend?" She confidently folded her gum over and sucked out a loud pop. I brandished my hundred-dollar bill in the air, the one that Daddy had given me.

"You can do a whole lot of damage in here with that."

She pointed over to a sales rack with her extremely long black polka-dotted nails, then nudged me from the back.

"Right over here, baby."

The hangers scraped against metal as she whipped the clothes around the circular rack by the shoulders.

"You a small?"

I nodded my head. "Yes."

Before long "Regina" held up a green-and-black broom-skirt and a loose-fitting tank top.

"Run in there and try this on, then come back out here and let me see," she said, nodding to the dressing room.

"Clean up on aisle four," she yelled to the clerk who'd called her Tonya.

Anything other than my usual blue jeans and tight T-shirts would be an improvement. After slipping the clothes on, I sheepishly walked out to take my measure in front of the angled mirrors in the fitting room. Not bad. I turned to Regina and opened my arms, making a "what do you think" motion.

"Wear those out of here, girl. That's a much needed improvement."

I took her advice and thanked her. She headed off toward the pet food section. We caught eyes again as I was waiting at the register. I waved good-bye with my ripped pair of jeans.

"You've helped a desperate woman. Thank you."

"My pleasure, darlin'!"

Up at the counter, I reached around and yanked the price tag off the tank top and then felt down in the waist of the skirt for the other tag. The high school boy ringing me up was watching, his cheeks went scarlet as he handed over the change.

Coming out of Fred's, I held the door open for an elderly man with a walker. He reminded me of Great-uncle Frank, and it made me smile. Outside, the breeze lifted the hem of my skirt. I felt a strange rush of freedom.

I spotted him way off down the sidewalk, recognized his gait before he was close enough to read the big letters on his "Keep on Truckin'" T-shirt. Darrell walked like he was muscling his way up out of the deep end of a swimming pool— his elbows bent, his shoulders swaggering side to side. He'd have made a good plow horse. His hair was cropped close to his head, shorter than I'd seen it before. Maybe the redhead was cutting it now. He must've spotted me too because he kept running the back of his hand across his mouth like he was wiping off crumbs, a nervous habit. About twenty feet away he started to mock the way I clutched the strap up high on my backpack.

"Well, look at you."

Too dumbstruck to say hello, I nodded and focused on the writing on the big sack he swung—"Becker's Army Navy Surplus." Probably stockpiles of fishing tackle.

"I mean it. Look at you, Penny Sue. What's happened?" There was a slight quiver in his voice.

Instinctively, I wrapped a tiny piece of my hair behind my ear. "I'm not sure that I've taken a serious inventory lately."

"I don't think I've ever seen you dressed like that. You look . . . great."

"Thank you . . . um . . ." I hesitated. For years Darrell had encouraged me to buy some new clothes and stop wearing what I bought in high school and college. I never paid much attention to how I dressed.

"Why are you looking like that?"

"Like what?"

"Penny Sue, you're not listening to me."

"Yes, I am," I lied.

What I couldn't bring myself to tell Darrell while standing there on the sidewalk in front of Fred's was that he'd lived with a ghost for those seven years—a see-through woman. I had disappeared long before he met me. Disappeared in that house I grew up in with my momma. Over the years, all her lies had a disorienting effect on me. I had lost my ability to connect with my body's intelligence, no longer paid attention to the butterflies in my stomach or the chill bumps on my forearms. I ignored sweaty palms or a racing pulse.

Somewhere along the way I'd unplugged from the socket of my intuition, from my God-given ability to read my body's cues. It's like all of the hidden truths in my house growing up had finally put my body into a deep sleep. I noticed that here lately, after reading Jebo's diaries, my gut reaction to situations had begun to return.

Jebo's purse was filthy inside and out. The bone leather showed scuff marks like grass stains. You wouldn't believe the mess in there: a pink powder puff, old Juicy Fruit wrappers, tobacco, gas and grocery receipts folded in half, song lyrics, and a little bottle of Elmer's glue. One day, Jebo had pulled a jar of peanut butter out of this same purse to slather up a matted piece of gum stuck in my hair.

At the very bottom of the messy bag there was a cloud-shaped ink stain. A Bic pen, half empty and still oozing, almost

dared me. I sat down and wrote a poem for Jebo for the first
time in ten years.

Her Purse

The church crouches in the crook
of deadman's curve, like an old leather catcher's mitt.

After the burial, huddled on the hill,
Daddy read the will, then and there.
My Jebo didn't have a lot,
but what she had was what we got.
She bequeathed me
her genuine leather pocketbook.
That bone bag dangled
off her wrist for years like a growth,
a bunion or something.

You'd a thought
she was hauling state secrets
or some other family's fortune
the way she policed that purse.
"Put it down" might as well
have been "Kiss my ass"
in that woman's mind.

Lumbering back to the car,
I didn't get far before

I knelt in the johnsongrass,
exposed this Tennessee tote-sack to daylight.

Chiclets spilled when I clicked open the clasp,
a vial of pills fell out on the grass,
Butter Rum LifeSavers, a narrow-toothed comb
ChapStick, shed keys,
a birthday card from me,
wadded-up Kleenex, half a stick
of Doublemint gum.

What I really wanted
was her rubber change purse,
sitting now on the floorboard
of the hearse.
It was red
with a slit down the middle.

She'd squeeze it open,
take her pointer and thumb,
press the coins down into my palm
at offering time, when they
passed the plate at church.

But it was there in the side zip pocket
where I found a secret
she'd thought she buried.
A love letter from a farmhand,

Howard McDaniel.
"I love you too" smeared in the margin
of the yellowed note.

Her purse gaped open
there in the grass.
Contents exposed
I felt like I'd stolen her clothes—
this woman who swore
she was never naked
before her own husband.

I think Jebo would be both surprised and proud of my
concoction. More and more I looked forward to the family
reunion.

～

The message machine blinked at me from the kitchen counter.
Lori Lee, my first cousin, had left a message saying that the fes-
tivities began around noon again this year at Uncle Billy's farm
over in Gibson County. The talent show usually got under way
around two o'clock. Uncle Billy had hosted the event five years
in a row, and he ran a tight ship. Uncle Billy catered dinner for
over a hundred folks. Momma and Daddy planned to meet me
there on their way home from Little Rock.

Every fiber of my being was gathering up into itself prepar-
ing, like a wild animal to pounce upon prey. Nothing could
hold me back now.

Sixteen

The weather report in the *Daily Courier* called for rain. I found Jebo's plastic ladybug umbrella stuck down into a decorative nail keg alongside Daddy's black one. I'd take it with me to the reunion just in case. Up on the wall above the nail keg hung a horse-collar mirror. My reflection made me laugh. I was a bedraggled sight in my costume: pink curlers perched like Easter eggs in the nest of my hair, Jebo's matte makeup thick on my face, her burnt orange dress tight like a corset around my waist.

Doctors always scared the daylights out of Jebo. But as her cough got worse and worse, she had to face her fears and go. Jebo said the only thing that calmed her nerves was to clean that horse-collar mirror by the front door. Every time she was getting ready to go see the lung doctor over in Memphis, she'd take the Windex bottle from beneath the kitchen sink, spray gobs onto the mirror, and use two or three paper towels to wipe it off. Didn't make a bit of sense; most often, Momma's mirror was already clean. But it was like Jebo wanted to see her reflection more clearly than was humanly possible. Mother despised her wasting Windex like that.

Well, I wasn't going to the doctor this afternoon, but for

some reason I found myself reenacting Jebo's strange habit, spraying the blue ammonia liquid onto the mirror, frantically wiping it off with the paper towel until there wasn't a spot on the sparkling glass. Only then did I feel settled and ready to go.

My car's muffler was dragging the ground, so I decided to drive Jebo's dull mustard Chrysler. Her car keys hung on an upturned horseshoe, nailed to the wall by the back door. I lifted the "Welcome to First Baptist" keychain off the rusted horseshoe and headed out to her car.

⌒

The hour-long drive to Uncle Billy's farm was a blur. I do remember, however, a Batesville Casket semi-trailer blasting its horn as I veered over into his lane and how my heart flopped around in my chest like a trout on a line. The next thing I can recall is the rumble of my car tires over the cattle guard at Uncle Billy's farm and the sight of his hunter green barn over the knobs of my knuckles, white in a death grip on the steering wheel.

Two little paper signs with hand-drawn black arrows pointed the way down a narrow gravel lane; the path was lined with tangled vines and led to the barn lot where we'd parked last year. Once I got there, another sign said "FULL." I made my own parking spot on the sloping hillside closer to the barn. Jebo's car would be fine there—as long as the parking brake held. From the looks of it, most of my relatives drove the

Ford Taurus these days. Aunt Edna whipped around in her late-model Pacer, elbow out the window. I waved; she didn't recognize me.

I climbed out of the car into the October air. The grass bowed down in the wind. Pumpkins ripened in the field; unseen crows cawed in the distance. Uncle Billy's prize mare, Babydoll, trotted the fence line. I yanked dry grass from the foot of the fence and offered my flat hand out to Babydoll, just like Uncle Billy had taught me years ago, hoping to lure the horse close enough to stroke the white blaze down her forehead. She ambled suspiciously over to where I stood. Her mouth tickled my palm when she lipped the grass, so close that I could gently blow into the dark cave of her velvet nostril. Startlingly alive, her soft brown winter coat was just beginning, thickest on her withers. She jerked away when Uncle Billy's voice boomed over the loudspeakers.

"Good afternoon. It's time to start the annual Pritchett Family Talent Show."

The sound of his voice startled me too; it was like my system had been set on fire. I turned and dove back into Jebo's car to calm myself.

~

The sun hid behind darkening clouds and thunder rumbled in the distance. My three precious diaries sat like well-behaved children in the passenger seat. I picked one up, scanned back over some of the poems; then, for the umpteenth time

I punched the buttons on the tape recorder to make sure it worked. All systems go—except for the cobra snake constricting around my throat.

"Dear Lord, don't let me turn back now," I prayed. I had to fulfill my mission to retrieve the fourth diary. Through the car window Uncle Billy's words sounded garbled. After cracking it open I reached for one of the cigarettes Jebo kept hidden in her glove box, then pressed the lighter in the ashtray. The lighter popped out quickly. I studied the ring of fire before touching it to the tobacco.

After the first drag, I enjoyed the slight dizziness. I sat there surrounded by smoke, a faint pattern of sweat gathering on the front of my dress, similar in shape to the gathering dark clouds overhead.

The softball game, called on account of the coming storm, sent teenagers hurrying back to the barn from the ball field hauling gloves, bases, and aluminum bats.

Uncle Billy'd pulled a flatbed truck up to the entrance of the barn for the stage. Inside the barn he set out row after row of metal chairs from the fellowship hall at his church. Folks still brought their own lawn chairs—you know how some people are. He'd spent the better part of his budget, real money, on a sound system. I mean, those speakers were huge. I hunkered down in the seat hotboxing my cigarette, biding my time while the Bradford clan from Humboldt got up to play their homemade instruments. Bobby Bradford strummed what was called the "john-tar," a guitar made from a toilet lid. His brother Harold accompanied him on the washboard, and their baby brother, John Luke, banged on overturned pots and pans.

Next up, my second cousin Benjamin Drury, from Momma's side of the family, sang the children's song "When Sammy Put the Paper on the Wall." Then some young man I'd never seen before, maybe early twenties, with a dark, woolly beard, ham-boned. His leg-slapping performance fell flat to scattered applause. Off to the right of the stage Raymond Hewitt's boys, little Raymond Jr. and Robert Samuel, swilled beer from the tap of the Budweiser keg.

"It's now or never, Babydoll," I called out the car window. I rubbed the bindings of Jebo's diaries for a shot of courage. "Whoever sent those fool notes to me better have their butt here somewhere." I had skipped around in the diaries so much that I had several entries left to read in diary #2. I opened it up to see if there was some reason I should just back out of this whole thing. There it was, underlined in yellow.

December 1966—Let it snow. Let it snow. Three days until Christmas. Porter had to put May Dean out at Bolivar. Nearly killed him to do it. We've seen it coming on for years. Doctors calling it exhaustion. Porter and I call it a nervous breakdown. Porter caught her trying to physically crawl inside the refrigerator, crying to beat the band. It was the last straw. He dropped by my house this morning and asked would I come stay awhile and help him take care of Penny Sue. Edna was real disappointed because this was her first Christmas without playing accordion.

January 1967—Bone-chilling cold. Phone woke me up at 6 a.m. May Dean screaming and hollering nonsense, "You're stealing my child, get away from my baby," at the top of her lungs. I had to hang up on her. She called right back, said she was sorry and would I put Penny Sue on the phone. It's pitiful. Penny Sue misses her momma real bad. Porter's afraid she can't take care of that child. After supper Penny Sue and I danced and sang to June Carter and Johnny Cash's "Long-legged Guitar Pickin' Man." Then I rocked her to sleep.

February 1967—Still cold. Edna wants me to come back home. Dr. Knight says she's fine there by herself. Penny Sue picked up my guitar today and wants to learn to play. Porter's working hard at the furniture store. He'd do anything in the world for this child. We had a nice visit with May Dean on Sunday. She's not crying as much. Does pretty good as long as Penny Sue doesn't run around and get into things. Porter asked me to move all my things to his house for good. Wrote a poem, in bed by 12 midnight.

February 1967—Felt like springtime. High 50s. Nice break in the weather. Porter sprang May Dean from the asylum. Doctor says she can't be alone with Penny Sue for a while. Porter's gonna break the news to her this evening. Penny Sue's growing like a weed. She needs her momma at home.

February 1969 — Freezing cold. May Dean threw her Bible down on the kitchen table last night. Made us swear on it we'd never tell Penny Sue she was at Bolivar. Threatened to kill herself if we didn't take a solemn oath. It was the Good News for Modern Man version. Funny thing is, I know how she feels. Felt that same way forty years ago when Edna was a baby. Back then money was tighter than Dick's hatband. I waited too long. Her fever spiked up over 104 for a week before I took her. Edna's never been the same since. It was all my fault. I tried to get the doctor's records burned so nobody would know. "Swear your oath on the Bible or it's no good," May Dean said. I'd never sworn to it otherwise.

Pink sponge rollers littered the floorboard as I encircled my head with a thick fog of Aqua Net Extra Hold hairspray. No doubt about it, Jebo's dress fit me like a corset. I yanked up my knee-high stockings, kicked open the car door, and shot out of there like a cannon fueled with a powder keg of adrenaline, her purse dancing on my wrist, the handle of the old tape recorder clasped in my palm. Jebo's bone pumps, strangling my feet, swished through the high damp grass; heavy dark clouds continued swirling overhead.

Uncle Billy was back up at the microphone making a few quick announcements as I crossed the barn lot.

". . . catered this year by Bozo's Barbeque . . . Now take all you want but eat all you take . . ."

121

I reached the edge of the stage, my head bowed.

"We've brought out two new porta-potties for your convenience . . ."

I planted one pump onto the stage, stepped up quickly and wrangled the microphone away from him. I don't know if it was the sincerity of my countenance or the hairdo coupled with the costume, but for whatever reason, Uncle Billy relinquished the mic. Bewildered, he stepped back off the stage, plopped into a nearby metal folding chair, and stared straight at me, mouth ajar. I'm not sure he even recognized who I was.

"Sorry about that, Uncle Billy." I cleared my throat into the mic. "Good afternoon, everybody."

I stepped a little too close to the speakers. The shrill crescendo of feedback caused the crowd to cringe and cover up their ears as I reared back like the spooked mare at the fence. Out of the corner of my eye I saw some frantic knob-turning by Uncle Billy's soundman. He glanced up and I recognized his toothy half smile: the UPS man. Somehow his being there seemed a good sign. I quickly moved more toward the center of the stage.

"I'm here today to share with you some poems by a woman a lot of you knew . . . Loreen Elizabeth Pritchett."

I held the tape recorder up to the microphone—the black rectangular box showing the tremor in my hands—and punched Play. You'd a thought I hit a button that caused a violent burst of light—because at the same time lightning struck close by. The flash lit up the barnyard. It was as if the good Lord was out there taking pictures and the flashbulb got away from him. The thunderclap that followed shook the rafters like a bomb had gone off. Little kids ran screaming and crying to their mommas.

A roar ran through the crowd. I must've crouched down on the stage at the sudden shock. Standing back up I took stock of my arms and legs to see if I was still all there. My feet planted firmly on the wooden planks of the stage, I waited out the pandemonium. Luckily, it wasn't but a second or two before most folks began to settle back down. A couple of scaredy-cats drove Uncle Billy's golf cart up to the house. Not knowing what else to do, I continued with my introduction of Jebo's work as a poet.

"I'm here today . . ." Before I could go on I locked eyes with Edna in the back row. "Hi, Aunt Edna . . ." I waved to her with three fingers of the hand holding the microphone and continued. She jumped up and down, excitedly waving back to me.

"Everybody okay?" I paused for a couple of beats before continuing. "I'm here today to reveal to you some of the poems my Jebo wrote." Aunt Edna was gesturing extravagantly, pointing at an imaginary microphone in her hand and then cupping her ear. It took me a second to realize that she couldn't hear me. Nobody could, except the folks on the first or second row. The lightning had knocked out the electricity. My microphone was dead.

"What? Not now, for heaven's sake," I begged under my breath. "I'm doing what I'm supposed to do."

A fire rose up inside me as my voice got louder.

"I want the fourth diary! Hear me?" I fairly screamed. My voice carried pretty well if I spoke up. Whoever wrote those fool notes was watching this debacle unfold.

I couldn't back down now. If I hadn't left the diaries in the car, I could have cheated and read from the books. Something ornery took ahold of me. I walked over to Uncle Billy, bent over to hand him the microphone, and then I reared back like I was up on hind legs, my front hooves pawing the air to quiet the crowd. My voice was much stronger than I remembered, coming from down deep in my diaphragm. "Thank Goodness, Lightning Never Strikes Twice!"

In my head I could hear Jebo cheering me on. Scattered giggling and a massive relief swept over the crowd. The words to Jebo's poem came pouring out of my mouth. I closed my eyes.

"White Lightning struck our house every night."

Truth is a powerful elixir, and I'd been drinking deeply from her well.

"A painful past'll make you a walking target
Kind of like a lonely pine in an open field—"

Great-aunt Thelma and Great-uncle Ralph might catch flies in their gaping mouths if they weren't careful.

"She should've been cookin' our supper
Instead of sippin' on a storm

Loved rubbin' the bottle
(Sloppily corked with a baby's sock)
Until the dominant gene, I mean . . .
The dominant genie of violence spills from her flask
And strikes our floor.
We wait on the thunder of her voice:
One Mississippi, two Mississippi . . . three . . .
'Feed the durn dog!'"

Each pair of riveted eyes in the crowd read differently. Some distant cousins on the next to last row looked dumbfounded, forks perched in midair, interrupting baked beans on the way up to their mouths. I'm sure I looked foolish, like a woman possessed, but I couldn't have cared less. I'd never dreamed in a million years that I'd lay Jebo's secrets, and my soul, wide open like this.

"Time, bump drags the knuckle of the long hand across dusk
You should have seen her after us.
Hair afire. A tooth or two loose
and black in the sockets.
Oh, the lady was lit.
We cower under covers,
pray for the storm to pass.
Lightning never strikes twice . . . my ass—"

Jebo's poem was revealing the secret genie of violence; once it popped out of the bottle into the stormy light of day, there would be no going back. You'd a thought I'd have felt a wave of nausea or debilitating fear, but what swept across my heart just then was more like red-hot pride. I was alive like no other time in my life, riding a fragrant joy bridging the wings of her words.

"In the morning clouds clear
The sun briefly shines
She draws a rainbow down around her shoulders like a
  striped shawl.
Here come the prepared promises, we know them by heart
'Never ever again, child, never again.'
A predictable path of crumbs
We follow into our family's dark woods . . ."

An uncomfortable stillness seized the air; even the boards of the barn weren't immune. For a moment the final words of the poem wedged in my throat. I waited, weighing our shared silence, my gaze measuring face after face. Aunt Kate's eyes matched her blue-checkered cowgirl blouse, her cheeks chubby and flushed. Uncle Bubba stared straight ahead, though he wasn't there behind his eyes. Hubert cocked his able arm, touched his hand to his forehead, like a salute. Raymond Hewitt's eyes sparkled. I think he was enjoying the unfolding spectacle. Aunt Edna waved at me and then winked the one kind, visible eye. I accepted each gaze like a gift, with a nod. Each one gave me strength to continue.

I felt the urge to step down off the stage and finish the poem out there beside them in the crowd. Shuffling Jebo's shoes upon the sawdust floor, I continued with the poem.

"Over the years I come to prefer my moonshine,
prefer sullen wool shawls made from
Ba Ba Blacksheep have you any wool . . ."

Moving toward the back of the barn, I reached out and squeezed the shoulders of Beth Ann and then Sheila Martin; second cousins, I knew that both women grew up in homes where alcohol had made their lives a living hell. The last few lines poured out quietly as I hugged Aunt Dixie, whose oldest son, Albert Ellis, was, right then, doing time for drunk driving in the state penitentiary.

"I prefer the jolt and the sear of White Lightning on my lips.
One hundred percent proof:
White Lightning always strikes
More than one
    to the floor."

Mission accomplished. I'd performed everything the notes had asked of me and more. Nothing in me wanted to hang around and explain myself—why I'd done what I'd just done. I made a path through the chairs, slowly walking toward the back door of the barn.

The humidity in the air from the coming rain made a mockery of my old woman's curly hairdo. I'd managed to sweat clean through Jebo's dress.

Just then I saw Momma and Daddy, Momma's face frozen in fear and disgust. She turned and stomped off. Daddy took off running toward me and scooped me up in his arms, my feet hovering over the cedar shavings on the ground.

"Now that was something, sweetheart! Without a doubt, a girl after your Jebo's heart." I wrapped my arms around his neck and told him we'd have lots to talk about back at home.

Opposite the stage at the back of the long corridor of the barn was another door. Uncle Billy kept it locked from the inside with an old two-by-four plank he slid through the handle. I wanted to go back to the car and rest. Aunt Edna clapped me on the back and said, "I have no idea what you were doing up there, but it seemed like a lot of fun."

Walking toward the far door, I passed by several empty stalls. I loved the fresh smell of clean hay. Uncle Billy had turned all the horses out for the day. The last stall on the right had Babydoll's name painted in bold black letters over the door. I knew Babydoll was out in the paddock munching grass, so I nearly lost my balance when I saw Momma's ghoulish stare behind wooden slats on the stall door, her hands clutching the bars.

"Come here to me, girl," she hissed through clenched teeth. "You made a fool of yourself and our family up there, Penny Sue."

"You okay, Momma?"

Momma's color was off. Also she had a white ring around her mouth like she was going to be sick. The hair at the nape of her neck was drenched in sweat. Her pinpoint eyes burrowed into mine like she was trying to possess me. Any other time in my life she would've been successful, but something fundamental had shifted. Instead of vacating my body for what I knew would be an angry onslaught, I inhabited every square inch. For the first time I found a bit of compassion for her. Before I spoke I swam around inside myself for an anchor to hold onto. Knowing the words that were about to come out of my mouth would completely change who I was in Momma's eyes.

"Get in here and explain yourself, Penny Sue." Momma's lips were quivering, her teeth still locked.

"I'm staying right here where I am, Momma."

I'd dealt with Momma's instability all my life. The difference today was that I could name my experience in the face of her lunacy. I took my sweet time and imagined a flashlight illuminating my insides, searching for something to moor me. There in the pit of my stomach I found an image—a copperhead coiled like a rope was biting off the end of its tail. The snake's head was shaped like an open book, black like the diary, creamy teeth like the pages. That booklike mouth struck and bit off the tail end of the snake. I interpreted the vision to mean we'd come to the tail end of Momma's lies. The image gave me warm courage, kind of like the feeling I used to get from a jigger of whiskey, but today I was stone-cold sober.

I let myself speak one of Jebo's lines: "If the heart won't break, the mind'll shatter in a million pieces."

With the image at my back, I felt safe enough to open the stall door, but knew better than to step inside. I would keep the door wide open as I spoke to her.

"I know the truth now, Momma. At least, most of it."

Momma held her hand to her mouth to steady her trembling lip.

"Jebo's left me her diaries, and she wrote down a lot of what happened when I was growing up. I know about your father. I know all about you being committed to Bolivar. You needed help, Momma."

My throat constricted as I watched her face go ugly and contort into a sob. Momma clutched the sides of her striped dress so hard that her knuckles blanched. It was like her fists were tent stakes and she was trying to keep her clothes from flying off her body and leaving her standing there stark-naked, revealing some heinous scars.

"She's a liar." Her voice broke.

I found mine again. "I can't take care of you, Momma. I won't keep my mouth shut anymore."

A grimace flashed across her swollen face. "Oh yeah? Well, as long as we're truth-telling, I've got one for *you*. Darrell told me that you're a drunk."

Her words stung like a wasp, but I refused to wince. "*Was* a drunk, Momma. *Was*. No matter what you say or do, you can't control my story. From here on out I'll be telling my truth. I might be all alone, but I'm going to tell it."

Momma slumped down in the corner of the barn stall, covering her ears. I only spoke louder.

"You think I could just forget all that's happened? In some ways I did what I did today for you. Hoping it might give you the courage to start looking at some of the ghosts that have haunted you all your life."

Momma wallowed in the sawdust.

I softened a little and put my hand on her back. "You didn't do anything wrong, Momma. Your life before marrying Daddy was just bad luck. You can't keep covering it up. Jebo told me everything."

Seventeen

Outside, the rain started falling. It was coming down hard. I waited at the entrance to the barn for a second. Evidently, Uncle Billy closed the talent show down after my performance. Said he needed to gather his thoughts and headed to the porta-potty. I overheard Aunt Kate saying to Uncle Bubba, "Looks like the apple didn't fall far from the tree." Neither one had the nerve to say it to my face, and for that I was thankful.

As I stood there at the back door, my heart still thumping in my chest, it dawned on me that no one was going to come up to me and hand over that fourth diary. Whoever had sent all the notes had hoped to make a fool of me.

What they could never imagine was the power and joy that surged within me while reciting the poems and how learning all those pieces by heart had changed who I was going to be for the rest of my life. I felt a sweet release from being bound and gagged. I'd said things up there and discovered parts of myself that nearly drowned.

Walking back across the field to the car in the rain, I realized I'd gotten what I came for, though it was nothing I could pull out of my purse and show as a prize. Jebo's poems, like jailer's keys, had freed me. By the time I reached the car I was soaked.

The ladybug umbrella eyed me from the dented hood of the Chrysler, wide open. I'd forgotten to lock the car. You'd think that, among family, things like this wouldn't happen . . . Someone had gone into the Chrysler, taken out one of my diaries, and just left it on the hood under the umbrella. The nerve! Angry, I raced toward the car, hoping to save the book from being ruined in the rain.

Jebo's shoes were slick on the bottom, so I skidded to a stop.

"Lord God Almighty, heaven and earth are full of your mercies."

It was the fourth diary. White paper stuck out of the book— sheet music for "Hard Times Come Again No More"—folded in half and slid into the first page of the missing diary. And on the page, her last entry:

September 30, 1989—Sunshine, beautiful fall day. I'm too tired to write much. I love you, Porter. I love you, Edna. I love you, Billy. And you, too, May Dean. And I love you, Penny Sue.

Make this one your own, Penny Sue. Write the story of your own life—the difficult one with all the beautiful details.

I couldn't believe my eyes. The notes on the page danced and swam. Every single eighth note in the song, shaped just like Jebo's soul—the dense round belly with an energetic waving flagstaff—was circled.

There, in the field, Jebo's spirit was alive with me. And for that moment we were together, and we laughed and cried and danced wildly around in the rain.

Acknowledgments

For their kind help and advice, I thank Eve, Kelly, Barb, Greg, George, Coke, Karen, John, and Molly. Thanks to Ami McConnell for her editing and encouragement. A special thanks to Coke for the use of his writing shack; and to my family, John, Jonas, and Liza, for their patience and support.

Reading Group Guide

1. Beauty has both dark and light qualities and often comes in dark packaging. Just as much of what is beautiful comes from beneath the soil and under the ocean. What are other instances in life where beauty is wrapped in dark packaging? Penny Sue was born loving beauty, though her mother seemed immune to its power. What is it about Jebo's poetry that is beautiful even though it often talks of the underbelly of life? Why do you think Penny Sue went to Beauty school?

2. Second generation violence exists in this story. Oftentimes what happens to the mother happens to the daughter unless there's intervention. At times in the story, Jebo seems to have a heart for May Dean, especially in the poem, "When You Coming Home Girl." Given their difficult relationship, how might this reflect a notion of beauty?

3. Jebo's poems reveal the healing quality of beauty once it has cracked you open and light can shine through. What do you think the impact of truth can have on a physical body? Does the lack of truth-telling have an equal impact on the body?

4. How does truth-telling influence how one occupies body and voice?

5. Penny Sue's transformation in being able to break through her legacy which was her mother's world and go further than even Jebo asked her to . . . (she was only asked to play the poems on the tape recorder, not to perform them). Once a woman finds a mentor, she may excede the wonderful expectations the mentor has for her. Can you think of examples of this in your own life?

6. Jebo is the character who embodies voice more than any other. What points to this?

7. How does Penny Sue's love of beauty draw her toward her life?

8. May Dean hid the truth. How did that impact her own life? How did that impact Penny Sue's life? Was she a victim in any way?

9. Jebo's poems spoke to and for Penny Sue before she was able to speak for herself. Who in your life has spoken for you when you couldn't speak for yourself?

10. At the end of the story it seems that Penny Sue has reconnected to herself, and dances with beauty in the field. What kinds of emotions did this scene elicit?

Available Now

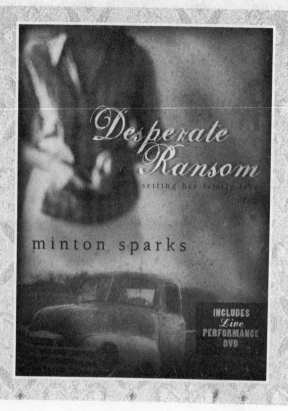

Nothing about the Sparks family was ever straight and narrow. In this collection of poems, Sparks introduces readers to the crazy, mixed-up, and always amusing eccentrics who populate her rural Tennessee hometown.